THE
Time
OF THEIR
Lives

**Center Point
Large Print**

This Large Print Book carries the
Seal of Approval of N.A.V.H.

Tales from Grace Chapel Inn

THE
Time
OF THEIR
Lives

Annie Jones

CENTER POINT PUBLISHING
THORNDIKE, MAINE

This Center Point Large Print edition
is published in the year 2009 by arrangement with
GuidepostsBooks.

Copyright © 2006 by Guideposts.

All Scripture quotations are taken from *The Holy Bible,*
New International Version. Copyright © 1973, 1978,
1984 International Bible Society. Used by permission of
Zondervan Bible Publishers.

The text of this Large Print edition is unabridged.
In other aspects, this book may vary
from the original edition.
Printed in the United States of America.
Set in 16-point Times New Roman type.

ISBN: 978-1-60285-416-1

Library of Congress Cataloging-in-Publication Data

Jones, Annie, 1957-
  The time of their lives / Annie Jones.
    p. cm.
  ISBN 978-1-60285-416-1 (library binding : alk. paper)
  1. Sisters--Fiction. 2. Country life--Pennsylvania--Fiction. 3. Large type books.
  I. Title.

PS3560.O45744T56 2009
813'.54--dc22

2008047595

Acknowledgments

Thank you to the editors and the many people at Guideposts who worked on seeing this book through, for all their hard work and dedication.

—Annie Jones

Chapter One

Spring this year was slow to arrive at Acorn Hill, Pennsylvania. It was late March and only the first shoots of jonquils had thrust up through thinning patches of snow. Here and there one could see the tracks of small animals that were moving about after their winter's hibernation looking for food and probably for one another.

Jane Howard, energized by the promise of the season, had begun experimenting, creating innovative recipes. These she proffered to anyone who came through the kitchen door at Grace Chapel Inn, the bed-and-breakfast she owned and ran with her two older sisters in what had been their family home.

"I can't help it," she told her sister Alice on Sunday evening. She had been at the stove the better part of the day, baking and brewing, stirring and stewing. So when Alice wandered in looking for a before-bedtime snack, her sister offered her a shortbread biscuit topped with a dollop of Jane's latest kiwi-jalapeño jelly attempt. "I just feel so energized by the change of seasons, so upbeat about the coming newness of everything. I guess that makes me a little restless to try new things, to be a tad more adventurous. To be ready for a, *um, uh . . .*"

"A bottle of antacids?" Alice teased as she delicately dropped the concoction into the wastebasket.

"A change," Jane finished, sounding every bit the peevish younger sister. Her youthfulness was her vibrant spirit rather than her actual years. The Howard sisters were no longer young women. Jane was fifty, though she felt much younger, looked much younger and could act much, much younger, especially when she thought her sisters were picking on her. Alice was her senior by twelve years, and Louise by fifteen.

"Well, that hot-sauce jelly is a change, but not a good one." Alice laughed. Alice had a wonderful laugh. Hers was the laugh of someone with the deep, abiding faith that no matter how bad things got they would, in time, work out for the good for those who love the Lord. And her laugh was contagious.

After a momentary pause to show she hadn't completely stopped her playful pouting, Jane joined in.

"It isn't supposed to be hot, you know. When you mix peppers, fruits and sugar, the result should be increased flavor, not heat." Jane gazed forlornly into the open ceramic jelly pot nestled in a lovely arrangement of biscuits and poppy-seed crackers.

It was rare for Jane to have a recipe go so awry. In fact, she was a chef of some renown, celebrated for her culinary creativity both in San Francisco, where she had been head chef in a well-known restaurant, and now here in Acorn Hill at Grace

Chapel Inn. Of course, as with any creative endeavor, there are bound to be things that don't turn out as planned. The important thing, Jane knew, was to learn from the experience.

"I wonder what I did wrong?" Jane mused aloud.

"Oh, let's not go in for the-glass-is-half-empty thinking." Alice gave her a pat on the back. "Maybe there's a future for your jelly, say . . . in the military, for making explosives." Alice peered into the pot. "You'd be surprised at how many things we use today that were invented by people trying to make something else entirely."

"All those awards for my cooking, all the rave restaurant reviews, all the accolades and never once did anyone mention using my food as a weapon."

"Well, send them some of *this* and you might get a visit from a government agent wanting the formula." Alice's eyes twinkled.

"It's not that bad," Jane protested with a laugh.

"Oh?" Alice stirred the small silver spoon around in the sweet-smelling green gel. "How much of it have you tried?"

Jane pretended a great interest in swiping away any crumbs left by the biscuit Alice had just bitten into so wholeheartedly.

"Why, you cheat! You haven't tried it at all. You used me as your human guinea pig!" Alice's surprise was tinged with grudging admiration. "And I fell for it. Just for that I really ought to give you some of your own medicine." Alice lifted a spoonful of jelly menacingly.

Jane laughed. "Wouldn't guests love it if I greeted them at breakfast and tried to carry on a conversation with a burned tongue?" She pinched the tip of her tongue between her thumb and forefinger to approximate the effect and said, "Ennjwoy the bwavothe wantcherwoth."

"Bwavothe wantcherwoth?" Louise walked into the kitchen just in time to hear Jane.

"Huevos rancheros." Jane slipped her fingers from her tongue and washed her hands in the sink. Over the running water she explained, "It's classic Mexican breakfast fare, though I don't think most of our guests would care for it."

Alice moved to the counter, poured milk into a mug and put it in the microwave to heat. "Especially if you made it with your newest creation."

"Oh, homemade jelly! I was trying to decide if I wanted to feed my sweet tooth or settle for something less dessert-like. This will provide a combination of those options."

Both Jane and Alice turned as Louise popped a jelly-coated cracker in her mouth.

"Louise, don't!"

"Wait!"

But it was too late.

Louise had already taken a potent sample of the jelly. She smiled at her sisters, lifting an eyebrow as if asking, "Don't what? Wait for what?"

"Uh-oh," Jane said, wringing her hands together and wincing.

Alice made a quick move for the refrigerator and flung open the door.

Louise shook her head at their reaction, or rather she started to shake her head, but somewhere between turning left and right and left again, she froze. Her eyes grew wide. Hand to her throat, she sputtered, "Water! Water, *now*!"

Jane spun around and turned on the tap, drinking glass at the ready.

"No, this will work better." Alice took the empty tumbler from Jane's hand and poured buttermilk into it.

Louise gulped the cold milk.

Jane offered an explanation that sounded lame even to her: "It didn't come out quite the way I intended it to, Louie."

"Don't 'Louie' me." Louise said as she dabbed the corners of her mouth with a napkin. "You only use it when you're trying to soften me up."

"That's not true," Jane protested.

"Is that so?" Louise raised an eyebrow.

"I also use it when I want to needle or tease you."

Alice stifled a laugh.

Louise smoothed the lapels of her baby-blue velour robe, but then, as though she couldn't help herself, she smiled too. Then she sighed and emptied the jelly down the disposal. "Really Jane. Spring or not, your experiments have got to stop.

What if one of our guests had helped himself to that jelly? He might think that we were trying to poison him."

Jane ruffled slightly at the use of the term *poison*. "What Louise means to say," Alice said, taking her place figuratively and literally between her two siblings, "is that while people love your inventive dishes, they might not respond well to something so, *um*, unexpected."

"I know." Jane nodded to show her understanding, then sighed. "But *I* crave the unexpected. It's spring, a time when I practically expect the unexpected."

Alice and Louise exchanged questioning glances.

"I don't suppose you two can fully appreciate my outlook." Jane pulled out a chair and sat down. Even in the heart of her home and family she couldn't help feeling a bit lost. For all the love and warmth she found here, sometimes she still missed the excitement of living in San Francisco. "It's this time of transition: not warm enough to begin gardening, not cold enough to snuggle down with a good book. I guess I take it harder than the two of you because . . ." She let her voice trail off.

"Because . . . ?" Louise asked in a soft, sympathetic tone.

"Because when the inn doesn't have guests, I have no real work to do. There is no one new to change the pattern of my day. Louise, you interact with students on a daily basis, and Alice, your work at the hospital means that every day something new and interesting is waiting for you."

"New maybe, but not always interesting." Alice leaned against the counter, her head cocked. In the low light of the kitchen her bobbed hair looked more brown than red, though in sunlight, the opposite was true. "Despite all the action they show on television medical shows, most hospital work is routine."

"But it has its moments," Louise said. "They *could* base dramas on some of the stories you've brought home."

"And a few comedies." Alice raised the glass.

"My sister, the playwright." Jane applauded softly to show her approval.

"Screenwriter," Alice corrected.

Jane tipped her nose in the air. "See, she's gone Hollywood already."

They all laughed, but it was clear that Jane was still upset. "Would you like us to pray about this, Jane?" Alice asked.

"Pray? About a simple case of change-of-season jitters?" Jane chuckled, but she was not mocking the idea. The sisters always brought their problems to the Lord.

"If Father were here, you know that's what he'd suggest." Louise held her hand out to her youngest sister.

Her restlessness seemed like a small issue to take

to God, this sense of wanting something else, something more. And yet, Jane knew that if she didn't find a way to shake off the feeling, it would grow and find a way to shake her. She needed change, and change would come. She had to accept that it would come in accordance with God's will for her.

"Okay." She slid her fingers into Louise's warm, open palm.

Alice took both her sisters' free hands, and they all bowed their heads.

Louise led the short prayer, lifting up Jane in the presence of the Lord and asking for God to work through all of them to make every season positive and productive.

After they said "Amen," Jane raised her head and let out a long breath. "I *do* feel better," she said. "Even if I still have no idea how to add some pizzazz to my life."

"What would you like to do, Jane?" Alice asked.

"As Shakespeare said, 'There's the rub.'" Jane sat at the kitchen table and rested her chin in her hand.

"Well, we're certainly on a theatrical bent tonight," Louise said. "You can't be the only person in Acorn Hill eager for spring to arrive and wanting to fill the time with something out of the ordinary. Perhaps you could organize something?"

"Like what?"

"Oh, I don't know. A play?"

"A play?" Jane shook her head. "The only presentation I've ever excelled at is food-related. I seriously doubt that anyone here is ready to dress up like pork chops and broccoli and trot out on stage in a production of *The Pageantry of the Food Pyramid*."

"Oh, I don't know. I was thinking that I might make an adorable strawberry tart." Alice held her arms out and offered them a curtsey.

"You must be up past your bedtime, Alice. You're getting silly," Jane said, laughing at the image of her sister prancing around in a red leotard with a crust-colored tutu. "Anyway, I would definitely cast you as a chili pepper. What do you think, Louise?"

Louise gazed at her sisters for a moment before saying, "I think a play might not be the best idea."

"I agree. I think Alice has the right idea: movies," Jane said.

"Movies?" Louise asked. "What do you mean, exactly?"

What do I mean exactly? Jane thought, then she snapped her fingers. "Well, I started playing around with new recipes because it's the time of year when we don't have many guests during the week."

"That's about to change, though, remember?" Louise automatically glanced toward the calendar hanging on the wall. "We have Ned Arnold coming in tomorrow. Heather Ann Hammond and her grandaunt Ida are also scheduled to arrive then. They are all booked for extended stays."

Again Jane nodded. She had made notes about the new guests, including the specific dietary requirements of the elderly Ida Hammond. "That won't interfere with what I have in mind."

"And what is that?" Louise asked.

"Just the thing to launch us into spring. Who knows, the coming season might provide us with the time of our lives."

"If it's all the same to you, Jane, I'd rather not be launched anywhere." Louise pulled the belt of her robe a bit tighter.

Alice patted her sister's hand. "What do you have in mind, Jane?"

"How does this sound?" She raised her hands and moved them through the air to indicate an announcement on a brightly lit marquis. "The First Annual Acorn Hill Film Festival!"

"First annual? Film festival?" Louise peered at the emptiness between Jane's outspread hands and pursed her lips. Clearly she was not seeing the vision.

"All right, it won't actually be a film festival, more a movie marathon. Or better yet, how about a movie club?"

"A club?" Louise asked. "You mean like a book club?"

"Yes! Only with movies! We could get people together to watch and discuss classic movies.

Maybe a few not-so-classics as well. I'll have to give it some more thought."

"You do that." Louise yawned. "Maybe if you sleep on it everything will come together and you can fill us in tomorrow."

Jane shook her head, unsure how anyone could be sleepy when such a terrific plan needed fleshing out. "Maybe we can get some sponsorship and do it up right. We could borrow a big television with a DVD player and have the meetings here."

"Now that's where I put my foot down." Louise stood, not to underscore her point but to move toward the door and off to bed. "We made the decision to make the inn a haven for our guests. We chose not to allow the irritants of everyday life to intrude on their stay here, including the noise and stress of a television. To bring in one for a personal whim . . ."

"All those new-fangled inventions just really get your goat, don't they Louie?" Jane crooked her elbows the way some crotchety old farmer in overalls might do. "Back in my day we didn't have no box with talking pictures in it and we liked it that way."

Alice smiled.

Louise raised her gaze heavenward, but she took the teasing good-naturedly. "I just think that we made a thoughtful choice and we should stand by it."

"Then stand by it we will," Jane promised. "I'll

talk to Nia at the library and see if we can work something out."

"The library? Is that really where you would want to hold meetings of a movie club?" Louise asked.

"Why not? Books are made into movies all the time," Alice said. "Seeing the movies might encourage people to read the books." Alice held her hands out like an open book, then brought them together with a soft clap. "And now with so much of the reference material stored electronically, and magazines and newspapers accessed online, the library does have a lot of space that isn't utilized."

"*Hmmm.* That sort of strays from my original intention of stirring things up." Jane gave a shimmy from her shoulders to her hips. "You know, I want to show something with a lot of verve and pizzazz. Movies from books might not have the right oomph."

"Oomph?" Louise's eyes opened wide in surprise.

"Maybe choose a theme . . ." Jane said, thinking out loud. "For instance, *um*, musicals." Jane snapped her fingers to emphasize that it was just a spontaneous thought. "You like musicals, don't you, Louise?"

"I like music." Louise batted her tired eyes. "Perhaps you can find a nice biography of Mozart or Chopin?"

Jane rolled her eyes and said to Alice, "She just doesn't get it."

"I think it's a terrific idea—showing movie musicals, not the Chopin bio-pic idea," Alice said. "It's a quick fix. Easy, no mess and you'd be bringing the community together for good movies and lively discussions. That should recharge your batteries."

"Thank you very much. I'm glad you like the idea," Jane said with a small tip of her head. "Now I'll just have to figure out how to organize things."

"I'm sure you'll figure it all out. And of course, the best thing about the idea is that this experiment won't burn our tongues and have us running for the buttermilk." Alice gave Jane a wink and a wave as she followed Louise out of the kitchen.

Chapter Two

Your work at the hospital means that every day something new and interesting is waiting for you.

The next day during the drive to work, Alice smiled at Jane's assessment of her thrill-a-minute life as a nurse at Potterston Hospital. *Every day something new and interesting?*

Alice loved her work and found it fulfilling, but sometimes, the drive in was the most exciting part of her day. She took in the early spring scenery. She'd made the trip so many times that she often forgot to appreciate the beauty she drove through. The one thing she never failed to do during her commute was to prepare for the coming work shift with prayer. It was a perfect way to transition from Grace Chapel Inn to the demands of the hospital and then back again.

This morning, she prayed for her sisters, her niece, her aunt Ethel and all her friends and neighbors in Acorn Hill who meant so very much to her. She prayed for her patients and their families. She prayed for the caregivers, that they would all be kind and alert, and for herself, that she would never forget that she was merely an instrument of the greatest Physician, Jesus Christ.

When she finished her prayers, she let her mind go to other things and began to wonder about Jane's solution for her springtime jitters.

At this very moment, Jane was probably at the library making arrangements for showing the movies. Or perhaps in her excitement she had jumped ahead of herself and gone straight to the video rental store trying to decide on the proper titles.

Jane wanted something frothy, perhaps romantic. Alice had suggested a classic, such as an old black-and-white Fred Astaire and Ginger Rogers film. She had always marveled at the grace and glamour of the pair and how they could convey romance without steamy scenes. *Those were the days*, Alice thought.

Ginger and Fred made her think of her own long-distance relationship, which wasn't *really* a romance. Still, the thought of Mark Graves dancing across a ballroom floor wearing a tuxedo made her smile. The veterinarian for the Philadelphia Zoo no doubt would use the outdated term "monkey suit" to describe the outfit. He'd also make plenty of bad puns referencing his profession. But, oh, with his heartwarming eyes and charcoal-colored hair, wouldn't he look dashing and elegant?

Alice parked and got out of her car. After taking a few steps into the aisle of the parking lot, she paused and looked around, seeing no one.

"La-da-da-da. La-da-da-da." She sang as she did a little step and a half twirl, envisioning taking a turn around the dance floor with Mark just like Ginger with Fred.

"Very nice!" A man coming out of the door broke out in impromptu applause.

Alice blushed.

"I haven't seen footwork like that since my late wife and I used to trip the light fantastic back when thoughts of tripping didn't conjure images of hip replacements and potential lawsuits," he said.

Alice accepted his compliment with a smile and a swift bow. "Thank you very much."

"When is your next performance, my dear? I'll be sure to bring a bouquet to throw at your feet."

"A bouquet? Don't you mean rotten tomatoes?"

Alice laughed and noted that the man, with a ruddy round face and a stocky build, looked familiar to her. "I don't usually dance my way into work. I guess I got carried away today."

"Nothing wrong with starting your day off with a little joy. Or ending your day with a little joy. Or infusing the minutes in between with . . ."

"A little joy," she finished for him with a smile.

"Why not?" He held his hands out wide. "You and I, of all people, should know that life is short. Time is fleeting."

You and I of all people? She almost asked him what he meant, but it was getting late and the man was a talker. He probably didn't mean anything in particular by the remark, but no doubt he would take two or three minutes and do a verbal tap dance just to tell her so. Then she'd be hot-footing it, not tripping the light fantastic, to relieve the nurse on duty.

"Speaking of time." She held up her arm and tapped the face of her wristwatch lightly. "I need to report to my work station."

"I hope you find a few minutes during your shift to turn that work station into a dance floor." He swept his arm out gallantly.

Alice laughed in astonishment at the notion but knew that at some point today, the mental picture of jumping on the countertop and doing movie-musical dance steps would overtake her. She laughed again, then said, "Something new and interesting every day," borrowing Jane's words as a cheerful send-off.

The man smiled and took a few steps back to hold open the door for her.

"Thank you," she said.

"No, thank *you*." He gave a little bow as she passed by. "I'd forgotten how little things can brighten a moment and even a small gesture of kindness can lift a weary heart. Thank you for reminding me of that *again*."

"A-again?" Alice had swept past him into the hospital and now pivoted toward him. As the door closed between them, she heard him say, "I'm so glad to have run into you again, Nurse Howard. I hope it's not the last time."

It was too late to ask how he knew her name or what he meant by "again" as he was already hurrying off into the parking lot.

She watched him for a moment through the glass door.

"Thinking of running out on us?" Nancy King, one of the nurses on duty, came bustling by with a stack of files on her hip and her red stethoscope dangling from one finger. Though new to the job, Nancy was known to nearly all the staff and had already earned the nickname "the Blonde Blur" for her quick pace and seemingly boundless energy.

Alice admired her co-worker's enthusiasm and dedication to her job. Everything about the woman from the smile in her eyes to the bounce in her step made her a delight to patients and a benefit to the other nurses.

"Now, don't even think of ducking out on us today. We have far too much to do and we're way behind already."

Alice began unbuttoning her coat and all but forgot the man in the parking lot as she hurried to keep pace with Nancy. "Sounds serious. Maybe you had better brief me as we walk. What's up? What have we got going on today?"

"Absolutely nothing."

Alice stopped walking. "Nothing? But you just said we have a lot to do and we're way behind already."

"That's right."

"Which is it? Do we not have anything to do or are we way behind already?"

"Yes." She gave Alice a teasing smile.

"Nancy, I don't . . ."

"Oh, I'm just having fun with you, Alice. I've pegged you as the kind of person who I could have loads of fun with. That's what everyone says about you." She took a breath and forged on. "Anyway, the patient count is way down today."

Nancy took a breath, and Alice took one with her. "So, tell me what we're supposed to be doing today."

"Everything," Nancy said as they boarded the elevator and the doors whooshed shut behind them. "And by everything I mean everything that we don't look forward to about the job: charting, inventory, auditing for policy and procedure compliance. I think if we get that done, they may make us crawl around on our hands and knees and test the electrical outlets by wetting our fingers and sticking them into the sockets."

Alice rolled her eyes and chuckled. "That sounds like the kind of thing my sister would have said."

"Oh? Is she a nurse too?"

"No, she's a . . ." Alice paused to think how best to describe Jane to a person who would probably never meet her. In a moment of whimsy, which this day seemed to encourage, she summed up her sister, the mover and shaker, with a word that suited both Jane's personality and Alice's mood. "She's a choreographer of sorts."

"How wonderful!" Nancy slung her stethoscope casually around her neck.

Ding! The elevator stopped and the doors slid open. "So are you ready for the most boring day at work ever?" Nancy asked, strolling toward the nurses' station.

"Why not?" Alice asked, sizing up the clear surface of the workstation as a possible dance floor. After all, when one worked at a hospital, one should always be prepared for something new to come up every day.

"Remember, keep your fingers curved and your back straight."

Louise's student, Virginia Wellston, was a self-taught church pianist. She had driven from Potterston to take lessons from Louise so that no one in her congregation would discover that she needed musical help. Dropping her hands into her ample lap, she asked in a petulant tone, "What was I doing?"

"Your fingers were straight and your back wasn't." Louise didn't demonstrate as she might have with a child, though sometimes Virginia's petulance made Louise feel as if she were dealing with a five-year-old. "As you know, Virginia, music isn't just playing the correct notes in rhythm."

"I've just always played the way it came to me, naturally and with feeling," Virginia said somewhat defensively.

"That's fine when you're playing for your own enjoyment or for family and friends." Louise took a deep breath and glanced around at her familiar surroundings to center herself. Just looking at the violet-and-ivory velvet piano shawl draped over her beloved baby grand piano, and the porcelain doll collection on the three-tier walnut table calmed her. It was important that her relationship with Virginia remain collegial. The woman was, after all, working in a professional capacity. She was here to improve her skills so that she could take over temporarily for her church's music minister through the summer. Louise continued, "But we are going to give you some more professional polish now."

Virginia patted her blond-streaked brown hair

distractedly. "I honestly didn't think polishing my skills would be this difficult or require this much dedication and commitment." The woman squinted in the direction of the fireplace, perhaps checking the time on the antique mantel clock.

"All worthwhile things require dedication and commitment." Louise waited quietly until her silence regained her student's attention. Then she asked, in a tone she hoped would make the woman think about her answer, "Why did you come to me for lessons if you don't want to change anything?"

"I want to change," Victoria shot back with a tinge of a whine in her voice. "I just wonder if I can. Maybe I'm too old to change."

"Nonsense." Louise sounded emphatic, even to her own ears. She couldn't help it. This was a subject she felt strongly about. "Life *is* change. It's not a matter of age. It's a matter of setting your mind to the task and keeping at it until you reach your goal."

"But I've done it the wrong way for so long now."

"No. None of that now. You're not too old to learn new things. You're not too old to want to improve yourself."

The woman raised her eyebrows. It was clear that Louise's passion on the subject of age and change had startled her. Louise had not intended to shock her student, of course, but rather she wanted to inspire her not to give in to self-doubt and fear of getting older.

Louise understood those feelings. She thought of the composition she had begun this winter, then laid aside.

"I watched my father age with such wisdom, dignity and, yes, even joy in every new day given to him to serve the Lord." Louise smoothed her hand down her navy wool skirt. "I'm saddened by anyone's throwing away the gifts of time and talent because something is hard or because it takes more concentration with each passing year. Come on, now, let's try it again."

"Yes." The woman smiled, nodded, then placed her fingers lightly, each perfectly curved, on the keys and launched into the hymn "Are Ye Able."

It wasn't the best rendition of the old standard that Louise had ever heard, but it was a marked improvement over the woman's earlier effort.

"Very good!" Louise patted her hands together softly and tipped her head in approval.

"Thank you." Her student smiled. "Do you shake up all your students with pep talks like that?"

"Shake up?" Louise tried not to chuckle at the very notion of her shaking up anything. That kind of thing was Jane's department.

Ding! The timer signaled the end of the session. Saved by the bell.

"Lesson is over!" Virginia whipped her hymnal off the piano so fast that she sent the sheet music beside it swirling to the floor.

On another day Louise might have suggested one

more run-through of the hymn, but today, she didn't have the time. Ida Hammond and her grand-niece Heather Ann were due to arrive at any moment. Louise had learned from her phone conversations with Heather Ann that her aunt was a wealthy woman accustomed to having people do her bidding. The elderly Ida had a number of requirements, and among them were peace and calm and quiet.

These were among the few things that Louise had felt she could guarantee without any problem. If the Hammonds wanted a private spot where they could hide away from the cares of the world, Grace Chapel Inn was the place for them.

As Louise opened the parlor door for Virginia, she heard Jane's excited call. "Louise! Come quick! The Hammonds have arrived and others as well!"

Chapter Three

Months ago, Heather Ann Hammond had made arrangements for herself and her grandaunt Ida to stay at Grace Chapel Inn. She had sent a specific list of their expectations and had called twice in the last ten days to make sure all was in readiness for their arrival on this, the last Monday in March.

"It's not that Aunt Ida isn't a well woman," Heather Ann had told Louise when they last spoke over the phone. "She's just not young anymore."

"Well, she is in fine company there," Louise had said with a laugh.

The young woman's tone was sweet, even wistful as she described her elderly relative's situation. "If it were up to the rest of my family, she would not be making this trip. They mistakenly think of her as frail and want to limit her activities. It drives her to distraction."

"Your aunt is quite fortunate to have you to stand up for her."

"Thank you. But if I seem to be standing up for her it's just because she never gives me the chance to sit down." The answer had come swiftly, accompanied by a soft laugh.

"I see, " Louise said. She liked Heather Ann Hammond already.

"My aunt is fiercely independent, Mrs. Smith. She's a highly accomplished woman who knows what she wants and has no qualms about going after it. I merely listen to her and try to keep one step ahead."

"Which is why you're calling today?"

"Which is why I'm calling today. I want to make sure our rooms are ready and that the details I requested have been seen to."

"I can assure you that we have been quite discreet about your arrival."

The Howard sisters were not in the habit of discussing their guests with locals or even with other family members, despite their aunt Ethel's often being in and out of the inn. She lived next door and was always curious about the goings on at the bed-and-breakfast.

Acorn Hill was a small town, and so word often got around about local happenings. For example, it was known in town already that Ned Arnold would be staying at the inn while he filled in as pharmacist for Chuck Parker, who was going on a three-week vacation.

Louise had taken extra precautions about the Hammonds, not even writing their names on the guest cards ahead of time, as she often did in preparation for arrivals. There was no telling if Ethel might steal a peek to see if she knew any of the expected guests.

Ethel might not have recognized the Hammond name, but if she had seen Ida's full name, Ida Lawson Hammond, on the registration card, she would have become more than curious. Many years ago the Lawsons had been quite an influential family in Acorn Hill. They owned a large business that employed many local people, and the Lawsons had been generous in sharing the family's good fortune with those in need and for good causes. Now Ida was returning with mysterious plans for the town, plans that demanded secrecy, her grandniece had insisted.

"We haven't let a soul know that you and your aunt are coming. You should be able to stroll into Acorn Hill virtually unnoticed." Those were the last words Louise had spoken to Heather Ann Hammond on the phone. Now Louise was rushing toward the front door wondering at the excitement in Jane's voice.

"Would you look at that crowd?" Jane turned from the open front door. "Carlene is over there taking photos for the paper!"

When Louise reached the front door and could see what Jane was describing, she breathed a sigh of relief. "Oh, Jane. Five people? That's hardly a crowd."

"In Acorn Hill?" Jane's eyes twinkled. "It's practically a parade."

Louise shook her head, "I think you're just trying to get my pulse rate up."

"What's the hubbub about?" Virginia slipped into her coat while bobbing her head this way and that trying to peer past Jane. "Has a celebrity come to town?"

"Well, I don't think our substitute pharmacist would draw spectators." Jane put on her jacket and stepped out onto the front porch, where she got a better view of Ned Arnold cautiously negotiating his silver foreign car into the drive.

The small knot of onlookers milling around the Hammond's luxury car hardly noticed the new arrival. "She certainly isn't leaving much room for Ned."

"Who is *she*?" Virginia asked.

"A guest here at the inn," Jane said.

"A guest who, I was told, doesn't want her name or her presence here known," Louise added.

"Sure doesn't act like someone who wants to keep her whereabouts a secret." Virginia stepped out onto the porch.

"No kidding." Jane said. "Makes me wish I'd printed up some flyers for the start of my movie club. I could get out there now and hand one to everyone. It would be great publicity."

"Publicity!" Louise stepped out onto the porch. "Oh, Jane, you can't know what a disaster this is."

Jane touched her sister's shoulder in gentle reassurance. "Ah, Louise, just be glad Aunt Ethel is feeling under the weather today, or she would be right there in the middle of it all, probably directing traffic."

"Please don't make the mistake of taking this too lightly, Jane. Having someone with the kind of connections that Mrs. Hammond has could be wonderful for the inn. A good word from her might mean an entire season's worth of bookings. We just cannot afford to be seen as ignoring her explicit requests."

"Ignoring? Well, no one else is ignoring her, Louise." Jane moved to the side and leaned one knee against the white wicker chair there. "If we're ignoring anyone, it's poor Ned over there."

They all three glanced toward Ned's car, which continued to inch its way up the drive.

"Oh my! I hope he doesn't park behind me and

block in my car. I have to get home before the kids get out of school." Virginia hurried down the steps, her car keys jangling in her hand.

Just as her foot hit the last step, a flash went off.

The student so eager to conceal her need for lessons ducked and flipped up her coat collar as if she were a movie star fleeing the paparazzi.

Louise thought of sermons her father had delivered about actions revealing character. No one here knew Virginia or her reason for being at the inn, but the woman had just demonstrated to anyone watching that something was not as it should be. You can't hide from God. You can't hide from yourself, her father would have reminded them. So it's best to always do the right thing for the right reasons and never have to be afraid about who is looking or what they might think.

With that firmly fixed in her mind, Louise knew what action she had to take. She had to do everything within her power to make this right for her guests.

In a few quick steps Louise was in the middle of the confusion. She glanced around and saw Nia Komonos, the town's librarian. Had Jane asked her to come in connection with her movie club? And there was Carlene Moss, camera in hand and obviously there on official business for the town's paper, the *Acorn Nutshell*. And Lloyd Tynan. The Mayor? Louise blinked at the dapper seventy-year-old man adjusting his trademark bow tie.

34

This gathering seemed to be an organized effort, a staged event. As Louise made her way toward the car, the driver's door opened. A young woman with long, dark hair and a look of utter dismay got out and rushed around the car to the opening passenger door.

Heather Ann, Louise thought, lifting her hand in that sort of wave that says "over here" or "I think you're looking for me."

The young woman smiled, but only fleetingly, then glanced inside the car, cocked her head, nodded and moved away again, heading for Louise.

Louise stretched out her hand, upset that their introduction would have to come in the form of a quick but most sincere apology.

"Mrs. Smith, I am *so* sorry!" Heather Ann said.

"*You're* sorry? Miss Hammond, I should be the one to say—"

"It's my aunt, you see." Heather Ann reached out and took Louise's hand. "I'm afraid she's pretty adamant about doing things her way. Apparently she had a vision of how this should all go and acted independently of everything I was trying to do."

"Oh." Relief flooded over Louise.

"Of course I should have seen that coming. My aunt does *everything* independently of what everyone else plans for her. Independent should be her middle name."

Louise smiled. She was going to like Ida

Hammond, she just knew it. "Then your aunt is not upset about the welcoming turnout? About all the fuss?"

"Oh no." Heather Ann pushed her hair off her face. She chuckled wearily. "Fuss is my aunt's stock-in-trade, Mrs. Smith."

"Please call me Louise."

"And you may call me Heather Ann. It seems as if you and I are going to be interacting a lot. In fact, I tried to call you a few minutes ago. I wanted to warn you that Aunt Ida had insisted we make some stops along the way to let people know she was here. But my cell phone couldn't pick up a signal."

Heather Ann took a breath and launched into further explanation. "When I saw that at every stop people joined in and began walking toward your place, I gave up all hope of this being a quiet arrival. I guess I should have known that anything regarding Aunt Ida could quickly get out of hand."

Jane extended her hand, her expression one of amused puzzlement. "Hi, I'm Louise's sister Jane. If you don't mind my asking, who is your aunt that she would cause such a stir?"

The answer came not from Heather Ann's lips, but in the form of Ida Lawson Hammond herself. Or rather her silver-handled walking cane, which emerged from the car. It waved about in the air to create some space for its owner and then landed with a decisive *thud* on the ground. Next came out a foot in a pristine white athletic shoe. The bulky trainer in contrast with the spindly black-stockinged leg made Louise smile involuntarily.

With only the older woman's foot and cane out of the door, Lloyd Tynan moved in. He offered his hand.

The cane waggled again, forcing him back.

"Thank you for your kind attention but no thank you, young man," came a voice from the car.

"Young man," Jane said and rolled her eyes in humorous disbelief.

For once Louise did not chide her sister for the reaction. It was amusing to hear the balding, gray-haired mayor called a young man and to know that to Mrs. Hammond, it was an appropriate designation.

"I can do this myself. If you all would just take one giant step backward."

The small gathering obeyed in unison.

"They forgot to say, 'Mother, may I,' " Jane said.

In the driveway Ida Hammond worked to unfold herself from the backseat. She pulled herself up to her full height, which Louise guessed was once nearly six feet. Age had stooped her, but in no way had it diminished her. At eighty-plus years, she still was an impressive figure. When she spoke, her voice, though it had a slight tremor, quieted the onlookers at the first syllable.

"Thank you. Thank you for being here today. I truly am surprised and appreciative of your kind reception."

"Surprised? Didn't she arrange it herself?" Jane asked in a whisper.

"That's Aunt Ida. She expects nothing less than that everyone should do her bidding but then acts surprised and humbled that they have complied."

"I am looking forward to getting acquainted with you and reacquainted with your community during my stay in Acorn Hill." Ida Hammond raised her hand as if to say she was nearing the conclusion of her remarks. "I know we promised this visit would bring good news and opportunities for many of you, but I hope you will forgive an old lady if she postpones the details until after she has had some rest."

"Mrs. Hammond, we are honored." Lloyd extended his hand.

"No. I don't think so." She frowned down at Lloyd's empty hand and wrapped her fingers around her cane.

"I . . . uh . . ." Lloyd glanced around at the group as if one of them might suddenly spring forward and interpret the woman's actions. Or his. Or just do something to make his frozen pose appear less silly.

"I don't shake hands. Germs, you know. Viruses and bacteria. Nasty things." Ida drew up her shoulders as best as her aged body allowed. "But in the future should you see me out and about and want to draw attention to yourself or to greet me, a snappy salute wouldn't be out of order."

She demonstrated by raising her hand to her temple at a jaunty angle, then dropping her arm to her side again.

Lloyd beamed and responded in kind, which enabled him to make use of his extended hand.

She hadn't actually suggested that their amicable mayor was disease-ridden, Louise noted, but she clearly had issues, and not just with him.

"First chance you get," Louise whispered to Jane, "call Aunt Ethel and tell her not to drop by. One cough or sniffle and . . ."

"And Aunt Ida might just chase Aunt Ethel out of the house with that cane of hers," Jane said.

At ease again, Lloyd took a deep breath as the red began to fade from his chubby cheeks. He continued his welcome speech. "Many of our citizens remember stories about your family and its many wonderful contributions to both church and civic projects. We are proud to have you among us again here in Acorn Hill and hope your stay is pleasant."

The small gathering applauded.

Mrs. Hammond acknowledged the applause with a pleasant smile and a nod. Then she turned and set her white athletic shoes on the path to the front door.

"Who is that?" Ned Arnold came up behind Louise and to the left of Jane. He had stayed at the inn enough times to feel almost like a member of the extended Howard family.

"Ida Hammond," Louise whispered over her

shoulder. "She and her niece will be staying at the inn. I hope it won't be an inconvenience for you."

"You mean any *further* inconvenience," Jane corrected, giving a jerk of her head toward the awkward way Ned had been forced to park his car in order to accommodate the town car, the crowd and the escaping piano student.

"I'm so sorry about that." Louise frowned.

The assembled group continued to stand in the drive, chatting.

None of this set well with Louise. Mrs. Ida Lawson Hammond wasn't the only strong-minded woman here with a penchant for ensuring that things were done properly. Louise could see that she had to take charge.

"Mrs. Hammond?" Louise took a step forward and gave a friendly but businesslike smile to the approaching woman. She didn't offer her hand. In her years as a concert pianist, Louise had dealt with plenty of Mrs. Hammonds, and they did not intimidate her. "I am Louise Howard Smith and this is my sister Jane Howard. We are two of the owners of Grace Chapel Inn."

"I don't shake hands." Ida gave a weak smile and a nod to Louise, then Jane. She kept her cane in a tight grip. "And I don't linger in front yards making small talk, thank you."

She moved forward, passing the sisters and Ned with her head held high.

"Yes, ma'am. Quite prudent of you, ma'am,"

Jane said softly and perfectly executed the salute Mrs. Hammond had demonstrated earlier.

"Jane, she is our guest and—"

"No, no. Your sister is right." Heather Ann laid her hand on Louise's arm to stop the gentle chiding. "She can be quite imperious when it suits her."

As if they needed further proof, the stately woman paused, turned and looked at the suitcase at Ned's feet. Then she pointed one elegant but gnarled finger toward him. "My niece will open the trunk for you. Please bring our luggage to our rooms as soon as possible."

"She thinks he's some kind of porter." Jane giggled with embarrassment.

"Certainly, ma'am." Ned gave a nod to the woman and turned to do her bidding, giving Jane and Louise a sly smile. "Glad to be of service to you."

Louise shut her eyes. This was going to be a very long visit, she decided.

"Oh, Ned, I'll get the luggage." Jane fell in step with the man heading for the town car. "You're our guest, you shouldn't—"

"Actually, Jane, I don't mind one bit. In fact, I sort of like being taken for someone who belongs here."

"Well, if you don't mind. When you're done, come into the kitchen. You've earned a piece of pie and some freshly brewed coffee."

41

"Thanks." He moved to the back of the Hammonds'car.

"Don't be too long, please," Ida called. "I have necessary things in those bags. Medicine and the like."

"Quite imperious, indeed," Louise whispered.

"Right now she's doing it for the onlookers, of course," Heather Ann said. Then she moved toward the small group. She told them that she would be giving more information about her aunt's visit to the paper later today. As the people began to move off, Heather Ann went back to Louise and took her arm as they walked toward the step where Ida Hammond waited for assistance. "She didn't just want them here to witness her arrival, you understand," Heather Ann said softly. "She wanted to set the tone for her visit. She believes this is a bit of last hurrah for her. She wants to create an air of majesty about herself and a bit of mystery about her intentions."

"She's a master of marketing then, because she did just that," Jane said as she trailed behind them. "You don't suppose she'd have some ideas about my launching a film club?"

"Jane!" Louise stopped in the path to look back at Jane.

Heather Ann smiled. "Trust me. My aunt has ideas about *everything*. And she is not shy about sharing them."

Jane was about to respond when she saw

Louise's startled expression and heard her cry, "Ned!"

The man looked up from the trunk of Ida's car just in time to sidestep disaster as his car rolled forward.

Virginia Wellston, who was backing out of the drive onto the street, got so excited that she began to beep her car's horn as if that would stop the errant vehicle.

Ned's car continued its slow journey, hit a bump, then went off the drive and into some bushes, where it came to rest.

Jane and Heather Ann gasped in unison.

Ned's face went red, his eyes dark with concern.

Mrs. Hammond yanked a hankie from her sleeve and dabbed her nose. "I hope this is not a foretaste of what lies in store for my visit. There now, young man, please don't dawdle. I take my medication on a rigid schedule and want to get settled into my room before it's time for my next pill. Be quick about it and there will be a handsome tip for you."

Chapter Four

I know I set the parking brake. I always set the parking brake. I *think* I set the parking brake." Ned said in a kind of litany as he sat across from Louise at the kitchen table, a cup of coffee before him. He slowly began to shake his head. "I didn't set the parking brake, did I?"

She opened her mouth to offer words of cheer, but none came. The truth was that the brake had not been set. She mirrored his head movement. "No. I'm afraid you forgot this time."

"This time," he repeated in a defeated tone.

"Ned? Is there some other thing bothering you?" Louise asked. "You seem to be giving this unnecessary significance. After all, when you arrived there was so much going on in the drive to distract you. It was an innocent mistake."

"Innocent? Yes, I suppose so. I guess it was no big deal." He held his coffee cup suspended between the table and his lips. "But there is a nagging voice inside my brain asking if it would still be an innocent mistake if the car had rolled into one of the people in the driveway. Your sister, perhaps. Or that elderly woman."

"Jane would have jumped out of the way," Louise said. "Or, more likely, she would have jumped inside the car, saved the day, then leapt out and accepted a hearty round of applause for doing it."

He smiled and finally took a sip of coffee.

Buoyed by her success, Louise continued, "And Mrs. Hammond? Oh my! That dear old soul appears to be so iron willed I fear if the car had rolled gently into her, she might have dented your fender."

He gave Louise a wry look and then sampled the piece of pie that Jane had set out for him.

As he ate, Louise relaxed in the ambience of the cozy kitchen. With its black-and-white tile floor, paprika-colored cabinets and maple butcher-block countertops, the kitchen surrounded its occupants like a heartfelt hug. It was a perfect place to regain one's equilibrium.

Ned set down his fork and said, "I know what you're up to, Louise."

"You do?"

"Yes, I can see through you."

Louise instinctively touched the top button of her ivory silk blouse. She was not used to being accused of being up to anything, much less to have someone see through her.

"You're trying to make me feel better," Ned said.

"Oh." She cleared her throat. "Well, yes, indeed," she admitted. "I suppose I am trying to make you feel better. But truthfully, the car mishap was just one of those things, as they say."

"Just *another* one of those things," he corrected. His breath eased out in a heavy sigh. "They seem to be happening to me more and more. Last month I forgot to pay my water bill."

"Oh well, that sort of thing happens to everyone." Well, not to her, she admitted to herself. But she knew it happened to many other people. An oversight. A slip up. "An easy fix, I'm sure."

"Yes. It didn't send my world wobbling off its axis, but it did make me feel upset when the second notice came in the mail. You know, people used to be able to pay their water bills right in my pharmacy, so I guess I felt a sort of connection to the process, and, even though this is probably male ego speaking, it embarrassed me."

"I understand, but I suspect it's an old-fashioned discipline, not just a matter of male pride, to always pay your bill promptly," Louise agreed. "Today, people seem to let their finances get in all kind of tangles. I'm sure that you dislike anyone, even a stranger, sending out a notice at the water company, thinking that you are the kind to ignore a debt."

"Yes, that's it exactly. Although to give myself a break, they had just started a new system. I probably only need to adjust to the change—old dog, new tricks, that kind of thing." He put his hand on his chest to indicate himself.

"Makes perfect sense to me. Change comes at us so fast. Think of all the things we've had to learn and relearn in our lifetimes. Why . . . why . . ." She looked around and her gaze fell upon the sleek cell phone Ned had silenced, then laid on the table so he wouldn't miss any calls. She gestured toward it. "Take the telephone for example."

"The telephone?" Ned asked, his fingers brushing over the gleaming blue object he had produced from his pocket a few minutes earlier.

"Sure. The first one I can recall ever talking on belonged to one of our neighbors. It was utilitarian black and looked like a candlestick, with the dial on the base."

"Really?"

"Well, you're younger than I, but you may recall the days when a man came out and installed your phone, and that was the phone you hung onto until it wore out," she said.

"Yes, of course."

"I suspect that was the case with the phone next door, though as a child it seemed a wonderful thing to me, even if it was an older model. Of course, nobody used the dial because it was just simpler to tap the receiver and ask the operator to reach your party for you." Louise rapped her finger on the table in the quick, demanding type of rhythm she might have used to urgently summon the Acorn Hill switchboard operator those many years ago.

"I don't believe I ever used one of those types of phones, but I've seen them in movies and on TV." He made a motion as if he were holding the bell-shaped earpiece in one hand and the heavy base of the instrument in the other.

"Yes." Louise mimicked the pantomime. "That's the kind I first recall using. Soon after, we got one of those sturdy varieties. It had a cloth cord and was so heavy you'd have thought it was made out of iron."

"My grandmother had one of those. Not to suggest that you are so much older, of course," he rushed to add.

Louise waved the thought away with one hand. "No. No, then as now, some forms of progress came slowly to Acorn Hill. Nothing wrong with that, I say." Suddenly Louise remembered Jane teasing her about her reluctance to embrace new technology. "At that time, Acorn Hill was so small we only had to dial four numbers to get anyone in the town proper. And for incoming calls? We had to know our special ring—one long, two shorts— because we had a party line."

"Now, *those* I remember." He gazed into his coffee as if he were seeing that distant past in the rich, dark liquid. "Maine wasn't any further ahead of times than Acorn Hill in that department. Though I believe when I was a kid it was just in the rural areas you found party lines. I can't imagine how the pharmacists and doctors in the days of party lines kept anything confidential."

"Oh, in small towns, I suppose everybody who was interested already knew who was sick before any doctor or pharmacist did." Louise thought of the prayer trees the church secretary had organized for children who had everything from colds to polio. And of neighbors calling in the middle of the night asking for her father to come quickly to a sick bed.

"That could well be true." Ned took another sip of coffee. "I know there were times when I knew about disease outbreaks before the doctors in our area. I'd get so many people trying to fend off whatever bug was going around days before they were sick enough to call a physician. Phones helped me out there, because customers tended to call instead of coming in and spreading their germs."

Louise smiled. "When we got our first really modern phone, you would have thought they had installed a space-age communications device in the house. It caused so much excitement. We had one of the town's first private lines, because Father felt strongly that what was spoken between a person and his minister should remain just between them."

"Even though they had been around for a while, when I first opened my pharmacy, I wouldn't have touch-tone phones. It was just too easy accidentally to press a button and disconnect someone while trying to write an order." Ned paused to demonstrate holding a phone between his cheek and shoulder.

Louise nodded, chuckled softly, then shook her head at the wonder of all they had been through with that one simple device. "And now people have these tiny phones inside of earpieces affixed to their heads, and they walk about carrying on private conversations for all to hear like . . . like . . ."

"Like they were back on the party line!"

"I guess that just goes to show that everything old is new again." Louise got up to pour an uncharacteristic second cup of coffee for herself and paused at the counter. She placed her hand on the small television they kept there to keep abreast of weather conditions and to watch the occasional educational program. "Why, just look at this kitchen. All the appliances, the modern conveniences that we couldn't imagine living without. Each one is something we had to learn one way and then relearn in the new and improved way, and then in the end . . . Well, you know, Jane grinds our coffee beans right here every morning just the way our grandmothers used to do."

"Except our grandmothers had heavy wood-and-iron coffee grinders." He made the motion of a crank, then took a sip from his cup. "But I see what you mean. It does seem that more than any other generation, ours has had to learn and often relearn and adapt more and more just to keep up with everyday life."

"And don't get me started on computers and satellites that beam information into our homes." She looked out the window and up at the sky for a moment. "That's one reason I think people choose our inn. They like the idea of getting away from all that."

"Yes, I agree. I know I find a certain peace here." His gaze turned in the direction of the drive where the mishap with the car had taken place. "Most of the time. I still can't get over my forgetting to set the brake. Or forgetting to pay the water bill for that matter."

Louise reached over and patted his arm. She knew that he wasn't truly concerned about the bill or the brake. He was thinking about loss, about time ticking away and taking with it things he considered essential to who he was: his organizational skills, his reliability, his mental sharpness.

No simple assurances from her could undo the damage that doubting himself might cause him. But still, she felt compelled to say something. "It's just life today. Too many things are going on. Too many new ways to do things are being introduced. Jane is always trying to get me to use automated withdrawals for certain bills, and I won't hear of it. To be honest, Ned, I'm a bit afraid of it."

"You shouldn't be."

"I know, but . . ."

"Jane has the right idea, of course. Keep up with the times. Stay informed. Never stop learning." He tapped his temple and grinned.

"Never stop learning, that's Jane to a T. You should hear what she's up to now—wants to pull together a movie club to, and I quote, 'stir everyone up, put some bounce in everyone's steps.'"

"Jane is always up for all of that—stirring, bouncing. I bet she keeps you on your toes trying new things all the time around here."

Louise nodded. Funny how the man had only been here a short time and already it felt like he had been in the inn for days. Regulars had a way of doing that, of blending in and picking right up as if they had only gone out for a walk or away for a weekend.

"Except for Jane, most of us are creatures of habit. We get quite cozy in our little routines and don't take to it well when something or someone comes along and upsets them. But if we give it some time and forgive ourselves for our own stubbornness, we can change."

"I suppose." He gazed again toward the place where he had relocated his car after the incident.

She arched an eyebrow. "I'm sure you set the parking brake this time."

"Yes. But did I lock the doors?" He chuckled. "Of course, in Acorn Hill that's not really nec—"

"Sound the trumpets! Unfurl the banners! Bring on the jugglers, the acrobats and the clowns!" Jane did not simply enter the room. She burst onto the scene and seized the spotlight. She held her arms up, palms out, the way she might have done when she had successfully completed a series of flips and cartwheels as a cheerleader in high school.

"Jugglers? Acrobats? Clowns? Don't tell me you've booked circus performers here, Jane." Louise was joking, but almost immediately she considered the atmosphere of the Hammonds' arrival and Jane's unpredictability and had to add, "Did you?"

"No." Jane waved her hand and crossed the room, her stylish low heels clicking softly in a way that made both Louise and Ned watch her every step. "Better than that."

"Better than clowns?" Ned chuckled. "What could that be? Tap-dancing plate spinners?"

"How about tap-dancing plate filler?" She did a quick step and shuffle. When she was done, she took a little bow and announced, "*I* have news."

"So do I." Louise looked down at the kitchen floor. "You've left scuff marks all over the floor."

"Oh, Louise!" Jane laughed and glanced down. She blinked in surprise at the black streaks left on the checkerboard flooring by her fancy shoes, then laughed again. "I'll clean them up, but don't you want to hear my news first?"

"I guess that depends. Is it good news or bad news?" As soon as she said it, Louise realized how silly it must seem to someone so animated. But this was Jane. She had a way of seeing an exciting opportunity to learn and change in any kind of news. "Jane?"

"It's good news and . . . *great* news!" She gestured boldly.

Ever the skeptic, Louise folded her arms.

"Well, if you don't mind my putting in my two cents, I'm certainly curious about all this." Ned leaned back in his chair. "And I certainly would welcome hearing some good news right about now. Not that it would pertain to me, of course, but it just would feel good to know someone is having a better day than I am."

"Actually, the good news could pertain to you." Jane rubbed her hands together with undisguised glee.

He rubbed his knuckle along his chin. His eyebrows crimped down over his questioning eyes as he asked, "Really?"

"Yes, since you are going to be staying with us awhile. The good news is that Nia has agreed to host my movie club at the library." Jane held up her hands and swept them from side to side as she said the words *movie club*. "And the library has all the movies on the list I came up with, so now all Sylvia and I have to do is choose two for our first double feature."

"I'm intrigued," Ned said.

"Having to do this at the library limits us a bit, though." Jane gestured as she spoke, her hands floating and drifting gracefully to accentuate her words. "We have to be respectful of the non-movie-club patrons by not monopolizing the facility for too long. And then the movies themselves present a bit of a tricky problem."

"How so?" Louise asked.

"Well, since we are showing them in public, we can only use films in public domain, for copyright reasons. I guess I should have thought of that once I wanted to do something bigger than just bring in a couple friends."

"Oh yes. That's serious business. You have to be careful the FBI doesn't get you. It's all spelled out in that warning that runs at the beginning of every DVD."

Both Jane and Louise looked at their guest in surprise.

Ned shrugged. "Hey, when you're a single pharmacist who makes the rounds filling in at small-town drugstores, you spend a lot of evenings watching rented movies."

"Then you are excused from coming to my movie club, if you have had enough of watching old films. I hope to get enough people in town charged up to make it an interesting evening."

"You shouldn't have any trouble doing that." Ned stood and took his cup to the sink, where he rinsed it and then put it in the dishwasher. "Charging people up is your specialty, isn't it?"

"One of them," Jane said.

"Well, good then. You have a project to throw yourself into." Louise sighed in relief. "So that's why Nia was here? She came to speak to you, not as part of that group following Mrs. Hammond?"

"Oh no. She was definitely here on behalf of the library. She was asked by Mrs. Hammond to arrange a tour of the facilities. Nia's being here just gave me the chance to firm things up regarding my plans."

"A tour of the library?" Louise asked. "Why?"

"*That's* the great news." Jane's eyes all but glittered. She lifted her shoulders and lowered her head.

Louise had seen this look from her before. Mostly around Christmas time when Jane was young and thought she had figured out some pending holiday surprise.

"I know what you're getting for Christmas." She would say in a singsong voice. Or "I found out who is asking me to the Christmas dance." Or even, "You'll never guess what secret ingredient I put in the turkey stuffing this year."

Louise caught her breath and found herself drawn into the delicious suspense of Jane's news. All the more so when Jane inched closer, checked the room for prying eyes and ears, then whispered, "I know what Mrs. Hammond is doing in town and why it might be wise of us and for everyone to get on her good side and stay there."

Chapter Five

A grant?" It was Tuesday morning, the day after the Hammonds' arrival, and Alice was trying to make sense of Jane's news. Louise had already heard all about it, but Alice had worked late the night before and her sisters were asleep when she returned. She didn't do late shifts often and this morning she remembered why. She yawned and rubbed her temples. "You're saying Mrs. Hammond has come to town to give money away?"

Jane finished the breakfast dishes while Alice and Louise sat at the kitchen table.

"More like a reward or a . . . a gift of gratitude."

"For whom?" Louise asked.

"I guess that remains to be seen," Jane said. She had already prepared breakfast for the guests. The Hammonds had taken theirs in the dining room but Ned, eager to get to the pharmacy and familiarize himself with things there again, had simply folded a fresh blueberry muffin in a paper napkin and hurried off to work.

"You know that Mrs. Hammond's family, the Lawsons, have a history in Acorn Hill, of course," Jane went on spooling out the details for Alice. "According to Heather Ann, Ida was born here in the early 1920s but her family moved at the start of the Depression. Do you remember her, Louise?"

"Remember her? She's nearly twenty years older than I and moved away years before I was born, Jane. I know you think I'm older than Methuselah, but . . ."

"Oh, that's not true, Louise." Jane dried her hands and hung up the towel. "I know that he had at least a couple of years on you."

"Don't even try to spar with her." Ever the mediator, Alice held her hand up. "She teases you like that to get the upper hand."

Jane came to the table at last and carefully laid a red-and-white checkered cloth over the top of the warm blueberry muffins that had infused the air with a rich, sweet aroma. "I really was asking if

57

you remembered her story, but to get back to Mrs. Hammond—"

"Jane, you know how I feel about gossiping, especially about our guests." Normally by this time Louise would already be in the office seeing to whatever paperwork needed her attention. But today, with the sun shining bright and the hint of not only spring but of this new turn of events in the air, she had lingered with her sisters.

Alice didn't mind, of course; she loved to have some time together as a threesome, sitting and chatting. It seemed that since going into business together they had less and less time to just be sisters. Sisters that, she conceded, sometimes got on one another's nerves.

"But it's not gossip, Louise." Jane tipped her nose up to show her disdain for the notion. "It will be in the paper tomorrow."

"Are you sure about that?" Louise crossed her arms over her prim cream-colored blouse.

"Yes." Jane leaned against the kitchen counter and folded her arms as well. She tipped her head and sent her long ponytail swinging over the shoulder of her vintage yellow and white sailor-style sweater. "Heather Ann read me the article they were preparing for the paper."

"Article for the paper?" Alice asked. She wore her favorite day-off attire, a pair of comfy jeans and an oversized striped cotton shirt. "That certainly sounds official."

"It has to be official." Heather Ann came into the room, apparently unbothered by the three of them casually discussing her aunt's plans. She had a single piece of paper in her hand and she held it aloft. "When you announce to people that you want to share your wealth, no matter what reason you have for doing it, you have to keep everything specific and clear—official if you will."

Alice looked at the single page in the young woman's hand. "Share her wealth?"

"Well, not all of it, but she intends to give enough to exercise caution in how she distributes it." Heather Ann stood close to the door. "My family is very well-off, you know. But one thing most people don't realize about the very rich: They can be the biggest penny-pinchers in the world. We don't part with a dime without due consideration, believe me."

"Heather Ann," Louise said, "as you have probably already guessed, this is our sister Alice." As Alice rose from her chair, Heather Ann crossed the room to shake hands with her.

"Yes, indeed, I did guess that. Nice to meet you, Alice. I hope the drama surrounding my aunt and her visit won't be too disturbing to you."

"Not at all," Alice said with a laugh. "As Jane can tell you, we all can use a change of pace now and again."

"I can practically guarantee that my grandaunt will at least give you that," Heather Ann said.

Alice's first impression of Heather Ann Hammond was a very positive one. Pretty, fashionable, well-spoken, wealthy, Heather Ann obviously "had it all," yet she was choosing to spend time in a bed-and-breakfast in Acorn Hill with her elderly aunt. Clearly a good heart could be added to her other attributes.

"I guess I don't really understand why your aunt would want to do something like this," Alice said.

"Aunt Ida hopes to find some worthy organizations and groups and causes to endow as a way of showing her appreciation to a place she still holds so dear in her heart." Heather Ann finished the explanation of her aunt's intentions with a warm smile. "I know she only spent her early years here, but she lost her mother shortly after leaving Acorn Hill, and her father was married to his work, so it's easy to believe that her childhood here was among the happiest times of her life."

"I see," Alice said, and she did. She could certainly understand someone carrying a loving memory of Acorn Hill for a lifetime and wanting to acknowledge it.

"Aunt Ida can be a bit off-putting, but she has a soft heart under that curmudgeon-like surface. There's a Bible verse she likes to quote when talking about her youth in Acorn Hill . . . it's about training a child . . ."

" 'Train a child in the way he should go, and when he is old he will not turn from it.' " Alice had certainly heard her father preach on that subject many times. "It's Proverbs 22, verse 6."

"Yes, that's the one. She quoted that on the trip here, saying that Acorn Hill and her mother had given her the training she needed to sustain her for her whole life."

"That's so sweet," Jane said. "Do you think that part of her wanting to do something nice for our town is a way of honoring her mother?"

"Very likely," Heather Ann said.

"I know!" Jane clapped her hands. "We could hold a reception for her. It wouldn't have to be fancy, just something to thank her for her thoughtfulness."

"While that is certainly a lovely idea, it may not be practical. At best, I have to ask that you hold off on anything like that until she's made up her mind about how she'll distribute the grants." Heather Ann stepped toward Jane and placed her hand on Jane's arm. "She doesn't want her judgment clouded by sentiment for fear of overlooking a truly worthy recipient who might not have the advantage of a personal connection."

"But this is Acorn Hill, everyone you meet has a personal connection to everyone else here," Jane said sweetly.

"While that's quite true, Jane, Mrs. Hammond must do as she sees fit. I think her decision is quite sensible," Louise said.

"Thank you for understanding. My aunt didn't

hang on to her family's fortune and grow the Hammond family's assets by acting impulsively. I do appreciate the offer, Jane." Heather Ann wrapped her arms around her midsection. "My aunt is certainly right about this town and the kindness of the people here. We've only been here one night, and, despite our causing a scene on our arrival, you still want to do this for Aunt Ida."

"What? That little kerfuffle in the driveway yesterday?" Jane lifted one hand and rolled her eyes heavenward. "That was just a flurry of excitement. It hardly qualified as a scene."

"Trust our sister on that, Heather Ann. She knows a scene," Alice teased. "And if anything, the splashy entrance only endeared you to her all the more."

"That's good to know, because I don't think Aunt Ida is done drawing attention to herself." The young woman glanced toward the doorway as if she thought her cane-carrying elder might suddenly appear there. "Still, she likes to say, 'Everything in its own time.' In many ways she is a very logical, methodical person."

"I know the type." Jane put her hand on Louise's shoulder.

"Oh, I nearly forgot why I came in here. Aunt Ida sent me to get some bottled water so that she can take her medication. She's a bit of a creature of habit."

Louise raised her hand and opened her mouth to

say something about that, then her expression clouded, as if she questioned the wisdom of defending a fellow creature of habit.

"She takes her pills every day at specific times."

"Your aunt certainly doesn't leave anything to chance." Alice had had plenty of patients like that over the years, but she never let their demands get under her skin. They were, after all, ill or injured and probably afraid. Maybe Mrs. Hammond shared those same frailties. "You need cold bottled water poured into a glass, not a cup, no plastic. I remember," Louise said.

"Just the thing for the woman who knows what she wants," Jane said.

"An admirable trait, I'd say." Louise opened the cabinet and withdrew a sparkling glass tumbler.

Slipping between Alice and Louise to retrieve a serving tray, Jane gave her eldest sister a quick, light hug. "I know I've always admired a certain woman who knows what she wants and isn't afraid to ask for it."

Louise shooed away her sister with a back-handed wave. "Pour that bottled water for our guest, please, and save all that sugary stuff for your cooking."

Jane laughed.

Alice shook her head at their antics, then gave the bottle to Jane and fixed her attention on Heather Ann. "So when will your aunt award these grants?"

"When she does everything: all in her own time." She accepted the serving tray, then excused herself.

"Imagine that! Grants given out for good works. I wonder who—"

R-r-i-i-i-n-n-g.

The phone startled them all.

Alice went to answer it. She listened to the caller's brief message, said thank you, then returned to her sisters.

Jane slipped into her jacket and picked up her purse and car keys, planning to run some errands.

"Who was on the phone?" Louise asked.

"I don't know what to make of it," Alice said. She should have known that neither of her sisters would be able to resist that kind of statement.

"What?" Jane stopped on her way to the back door, her car keys dangling from her fingers.

"Nothing is amiss, I hope?" Louise asked.

"Amiss? No. That was an administrative assistant from the hospital. She just wanted me to know that I have received a delivery there today. She said they'd normally have just held it for me, but . . ."

"But what, Alice? You're starting to talk like Jane."

"Hey!" Jane shot Louise a pretend annoyed look, then turned to Alice. "What's up? Something mysterious? Puzzling? Or better yet, romantic?"

"Romantic? Why would you say that?" Alice asked.

"A delivery that makes the staff take notice? It sounds possibly romantic to me." Jane put her hand over her heart inside her jacket and raised and lowered it to mimic a beating heart. "Do you think it's from Mark?"

Mark sending something to her at the hospital? It didn't seem likely. She and Mark shared many common sensibilities, from their devotion to their work to their love of the Lord. They both cherished their special friendship, but outward displays of sentimentality for no reason were just not a part of it.

"No, I don't think they're from Mark."

"They?" Louise slid the paper she had been studying to the side. "Just what was delivered to the hospital, Alice?"

"Flowers."

"Oh, flowers!" Jane gave a wave. "What's so special about that? You've gotten flowers at the hospital before, haven't you?"

"Yes, I've received flowers as a thank-you from patients from time to time, but I got the distinct feeling these are different somehow."

"How?" Jane's keys jingled softly.

"Apparently the envelope for the card that came with the arrangement, for starters."

"What could be so special about an envelope?"

"It is very elegant vellum with an embossed rose on the flap."

"Ooh-la-la!" Jane raised her eyebrows. "That

doesn't sound like your run-of-the-mill thank-you."

"No, it doesn't. The caller also seemed rather impressed with the bouquet. She said it would be an awful waste to leave them to wilt until my next shift."

"Then you have to go and see for yourself." Jane did not offer it as a suggestion but as a statement of fact. "Get your coat. I was on my way to Potterston anyway."

"I thought you were going to the bank, then to find some decorations for that first movie club event."

"Yes, Nia said we could put up some posters and things to set the mood. I was going to just see what I could find around town, but I had it in the back of my head that I should drive to Potterston and hit a few video rental places."

"Jane, the back of your head must be a very fascinating place, all the things you have stored back there." Alice sighed. "I thought the library had plenty of movies for your event, why do you want to go to rental places?"

"Because sometimes they let you have the posters and promotional cardboard props once they are done with them. Doesn't that sound terrific? Cutouts of movie characters and posters to hang in the library window?"

"I hope those things will look better in the library than they do staring out the backseat windows of your car." Alice eyed the cardboard cutout of a pirate and the big pink tongue of a shaggy dog visible on the rolled-up posters leaning against the driver's-side seat.

"You didn't mind my stopping in to ask about this stuff before we went to the hospital, did you?" Jane asked. "I just thought that if your flowers are in a vase . . ."

"I know. You didn't want to have them wilting or falling over while we hopped in and out of the car trying to hit the freebie-movie-themed jackpot."

"You sound more like me every day." Jane laughed. "I think my moving back here has been a good influence on you, Alice."

"Well, you certainly keep me busy."

"Speaking of keeping busy, will you look at that?" Jane took her hand off the wheel only long enough to point.

"What?" Alice leaned as far forward as the seatbelt would allow. "The fast-food place promising new healthier french fries in two larger sizes? Shoe repair while we wait? Antiques and collectibles? Zero financing on washer and dryer units?"

"That sign there." She indicated a brick building with a sandwich-board sign propped up beside the heavy double doors. "Outside the Whole Family Learning Annex."

"Learn to dance." Alice obliged her sister by reading the sign aloud as they drove slowly past. "Ballroom. Swing. Salsa. Classes starting soon."

Jane removed a small pad of yellow paper with a pen clipped to it from the sun visor and waved it in Alice's general direction. "Jot down the number for me, will you?"

"Why do you want that number?" Alice asked.

"Because I might want to give it a try."

Alice scribbled fast.

Jane only hoped the numbers would be readable later.

"You? Really? Ballroom dancing? That's more Louise's area, isn't it?"

"Well, actually, I'm thinking maybe salsa would suit me better, don't you think? Sassy, spicy . . ."

"Sometimes a real dip."

"Alice! Good one." Jane wriggled behind the wheel, making her ponytail bounce. "I *am* a good influence on you after all."

They didn't stop laughing and kidding each other until they got to the hospital. There Alice requested that they put on serious faces. As long as they were within view or earshot of anyone who worked at or might be a patient at the hospital, she insisted they behave with dignity.

It took no effort for Alice. It seemed the moment she walked through the doors, Alice slipped into her professional demeanor. Of course Jane had always admired her older sister but never more so than when she saw her in her role as the kind of nurse everyone counted on and sought comfort from. It was a gift, the ability and desire to help and heal, and Alice embodied that gift and that commission in words, deeds and with her whole heart.

When they inquired about the flowers, they learned that the arrangement had been sent to Alice's workstation.

"That must be some unusual floral arrangement," Jane commented. "Everyone seems to know about it."

With every step toward the workstation, a reddish flush crept higher up Alice's neck. Jane saw her sister's discomfort. Alice simply did not like to be the center of attention like this.

"You should just get the flowers and go. Don't even read the card, or everyone will want to find out who sent them," Jane whispered.

"I'm sure it's just a thank-you from a patient, Jane. As you said, I've gotten flowers here before. No big deal." Alice sounded calm and confident, but the flush, which had now reached her cheeks, gave her away.

As they neared Alice's workstation, Nancy King popped up from a seat behind it. "Oh, Alice! What a surprise to see you here today!" Nancy gave the sisters her high-wattage smile. "You're not subbing for someone today, are you?" She turned to Jane. "I haven't been working here all that long. Came here after I lost my husband Ray last year. Wanted to make a fresh start, you know how that is."

Jane nodded. She did know how that was. She just didn't know how to respond to a stranger blurting things out like that in a workplace. Jane wondered if she should respond or just smile and wait for her sister to take the lead. Nancy solved her dilemma by continuing her one-sided conversation.

"Anyway," Nancy rushed on, "my daughter is going to have a baby. My first grandbaby. It breaks my heart that Ray didn't live to see that day, but that was God's will, I tell myself."

Jane saw Alice open her mouth, but whether her sister planned to agree with the woman or to interrupt her, Jane would never know, for Nancy drew a quick breath and forged on. "But I've gotten off track. What I wanted to say was that when my daughter goes into labor I'm going to need a sub, maybe on very short notice because babies, well, you know they don't like to arrive on schedule."

And your point is? Jane wanted to ask the vivacious woman, but she had promised Alice she would be on her best behavior so she stood there quietly watching the scene unfold.

Nancy finally seemed to be heading for the end of her tale. *And "*—and this is what I was getting at when I asked about your subbing—everyone here at the hospital said that I should ask you if you could sub in a real pinch, because everyone says you are such a doll."

"I'd be happy to help you if you need me and if

I'm not already on the schedule, of course." Alice's shoulders relaxed and she shut her eyes as if she really believed they had sorted that all out and she could now deal with her own issue.

"Great!" Nancy smacked her hands down on the counter, nearly sending a stack of charts off the edge. "Because what's more, everyone says they love to work with you and know you will come in prepared, not like some folks, who show up all out of sorts because it's not their regular shift. So?"

"So?" Alice frowned.

"So, are you subbing today?"

"Oh. No. No, Nancy. Not today. I just came in with my sister—"

"Oh! Your sister, the choreographer!" Nancy waved the patient file in her hand. "I've never met a choreographer before in my entire life. At least not that I know of, though with all the patients I've taken care of in my career, you never know. Do you?"

"Choreographer?" Jane was bewildered. "But I'm a—"

"She's a very busy woman." Alice shot Jane a bemused glance that promised she would explain it all later. "I just dropped by because they called me and said I had a—"

"The flowers! Oh my, yes! I was here when they arrived, and let me tell you they are gorgeous." She batted at the air even as she changed direction and headed for the back of the nurses' station.

"Somebody sure likes you, Alice. I wish I had someone in my life who would lavish something like this on me, and to send them to you at work where everyone can see them, I don't know who he is but he is a keeper."

"He?" Alice's flush suddenly deepened.

"You don't think she read the card, do you?" Jane whispered.

"Hang on a sec, I'll get those flowers for you," Nancy said. "Then you have to stand right here and read the card. Everyone is dying to know who they are from."

"Should she use a phrase like 'dying to know' in a hospital?" Jane asked.

"Dignity," Alice reminded Jane.

"If you read the card *here*, within the hour everyone in the hospital and halfway across the state will know who they are from and how you feel," Jane warned in a low and decidedly digni-fied tone. "You have got to get those flowers from her and get out. In a dignified manner, of course."

"Of course," Alice echoed.

"Here they are! Stunning, aren't they?" Nancy held aloft a tall, fluted crystal vase, elegant and modern in design, filled with a tall bouquet of yellow tulips, lavender iris, pink-tinged peonies and one perfect calla lily.

"Wow," Jane said in admiration. Then she said quietly, just for Alice to hear, "An arrangement like that had to have cost a small fortune."

"Well?" Nancy plucked the card from its plastic spike and held it out in Alice's direction. "Aren't you going to read the card?"

By this time two other nurses and a patient were gathered around the station. Jane couldn't tell if they were there to check charts or to witness the opening of the card.

"I, *um* . . ." Alice took the card from Nancy and, in her haste to leave, shoved it into the vase. "I think I'll just grab these and go." Alice took the flowers away from the other nurse.

"But aren't you going to—" Nancy began to ask.

Alice smiled, then said firmly, "I'd really prefer to open the card in private. Thanks so much for keeping the flowers safe." Then she turned and started down the hall with Jane following at her heels.

When they turned a corner and were out of view, Jane said, "Alice, stop! You've got the card wet. Grab it before the ink runs and we can't read the name of your secret admirer."

Chapter Six

Where should I put these flowers, Louise?" Alice asked as she carried the vase into the kitchen Wednesday morning.

"Don't you want them in your room any longer?"

When she and Jane returned from Potterston, Alice had taken the arrangement to her room in the hope that keeping them out of sight would avoid questions about who sent them and why. But today, she decided that the lovely flowers should be displayed where everyone could enjoy them.

"I thought I should share them. They are so lovely," she told her sister.

"Do you know anything more about Mr. . . . Mr. . . ."

"Dover. Abraham Dover," Alice reminded her, and even as she said the name she wondered who he was. She simply could not place the name.

Jane's quick retrieval of the card from the water-logged envelope didn't save the message. In fact, only part of the name was legible. The first name started with an *A*, but the rest was a blur of letters. The last name was "Dove . . ." something. That gave them enough information, however, to call the florist listed on the card and to ask the name of the sender. Abraham Dover, or Abe, the woman had told them. He had dithered over whether Alice would remember him best as Abraham or Abe.

He shouldn't have concerned himself, Alice thought, *I don't remember him with either name.* For the life of her, she still could not picture this Abe Dover or fathom why he would have sent her these flowers.

"Did the florist tell you how to contact Mr. Dover? Maybe you could just call him and ask why he sent the flowers." Louise took the vase from Alice's hands and set it in the sink to add some water and to pinch off a few bits of broken and dried-out greenery.

"They couldn't give me that information." Alice looked at the clock and realized Heather Ann would be down soon for her aunt's bottled water.

"You asked?" Louise shook water droplets from a stem of eucalyptus leaves.

Alice went to the refrigerator for a water bottle, which she set on the table, then she went to the cabinet for a drinking glass.

"Jane did," Alice told her. "But he paid with cash, so they didn't have an address for him."

"*Hmmm.*"

"Jane also suggested that maybe I could get a clue about the man who sent them from the kind of flowers he chose."

"Interesting theory." Louise paused. She tapped her fingertip to her chin. "The Victorians had an entire language of flowers. Perhaps your Mr. Dover might have sent a message with these flowers."

"He is not *my* Mr. Dover." Alice put down the glass on the tray they provided for Mrs. Hammond's morning ritual. "But I guess it wouldn't hurt to try to decipher something about him by studying that bouquet." Alice reached in the pocket of her green sweater jacket and pulled out a piece of paper. "Jane went on the Internet and printed off this list of what each flower means. Let's see, iris means 'faith, hope, wisdom.' "

"Well, you are very wise and certainly you are faithful and hopeful," Louise interjected.

"Yes . . . well, yellow tulips mean—oh dear!—'hopeless love.'"

"Oh my!"

"And calla lilies represent 'beauty.' Oh, this is silly. It's getting us nowhere."

"Maybe the message is simpler than all that," Louise suggested. "Maybe it's meant to remind you of something."

Alice shrugged. "All right, then, let's study this arrangement and see what we can come up with."

Louise took a step back. "One calla lily."

"We're interpreting, Louise, not taking inventory," Alice said with a laugh. She folded her arms and tipped her head to the right a bit, as if that shift in point of view might just be the thing to uncover something neither of them had noticed before. "Let me just . . . let me just take them in for a moment before we start throwing ideas around."

They both stood there in silence for several seconds.

"They're lovely," Louise finally said. "That much we know."

Alice had to admit that they were beautiful, particularly with the morning sun shining on them. And she noticed that their wonderful, subtle scent was perfuming the air.

"Now let's see." Louise touched one open yellow petal. "We have tulips. Tulips come from

Holland originally. Do you know anyone from Holland?"

"No, Louise. And the eucalyptus filler comes from Australia and I don't know anyone from Australia either, at least in connection with any Abe Dover."

"Okay." Louise narrowed her eyes and moved in to study the arrangement more closely. She touched the flowers and even ran her fingertip around the rim of the vase. Finally she stood back, sighed and said, "I guess there's only one other thing that comes to mind. Do you know anyone named Lily?"

"Do I . . . ?" Alice sighed, pondered Louise's question and then threw her hands up in the air. "Oh, Louise, I can't think of anyone named Lily, but why would a man—"

"Abraham Dover."

"Yes, why would Abraham Dover send me, *Alice*, a floral arrangement with a flower bearing the name of another woman?"

"Lily," Louise helpfully supplied.

"Yes, yes. Lily." Alice stared at the single white flower at the center of the arrangement. "I'm Alice. He's Abraham Dover. And Lily is . . ." Alice caught her breath. A light went on in her mind. She laughed, lightly. "Could it really be that simple? Of course it could!"

"You remember, don't you?"

"You are brilliant, Louise. Lily is Lillian Dover."

"Well, there you have it." Louise beamed with pride. "So, now, who is Lillian Dover and why would Abraham send *you* flowers at the hospital?"

"She was my patient. She had a very long stay in the hospital and she put up a valiant struggle to recover, but in the end . . ."

Alice shook her head sadly. Alice had always felt that her calling was both a blessing and a burden. It demanded a strong constitution, a clear head and most of all, a tender heart. And sometimes, those qualities came into conflict when dealing with people who were suffering, who were confused and even despairing. Alice knew what to do and carried out each necessary task without hesitation. But her heart ached for her patients and their loved ones.

Early in her career, Alice had begun to rely on the verse in Proverbs about a cheery heart doing good, like a medicine. She understood that her attitude might just be the thing that rallied a patient enough to keep going that day. Or, that hers might be the last touch of human kindness a patient experienced before death overtook him or her.

But in the end, like every other nurse that Alice knew, she carried in her heart the sorrow of losing a patient. Every life counted. Every person mattered.

Louise remained silent. She could sense that Alice was mentally revisiting Lillian Dover's last days. She was just about to offer a comforting hug when the sharp ring of the telephone broke the silence in the room. She moved toward the phone, muttering something that sounded like "not another one."

Alice looked at the floral arrangement with new understanding. She recalled Lillian Dover and, to a lesser degree, her husband of many years, Abe. What she recalled most about him was the way his wife's prolonged illness had taken its toll on his body and mind. He had become more stooped and his skin appeared to have become gray. *Bleak* was the way she would have described him back then. And yet he had an inner light that appeared whenever he spoke tenderly to his dying wife.

Lillian had come in already long past medical science's ability to save her. But miracles do happen and it is always too soon to give up hope, so Alice had put on a smile and given the woman the same attention and care that she would give a patient she knew would go home healthy.

Early in her career, Alice had gone to a seminar given by a hospice nurse who admonished them, "There is no lesser degree of patient. There are only two kinds of patients you will ever minister to—the living and the dead. You must treat all your patients as living beings until they pass into that second category."

Alice had promised herself then she would always do just that. In dealing with Lillian Dover, she had tried to make the woman comfortable. She had made sure her patient had a little sunshine each day, and when she learned that Lillian loved classical music, she had asked Louise for some advice on uplifting choices, then took in a portable CD player so Lillian's room could be filled with Mozart, Beethoven and other beautiful music.

And now Abe had sent her this arrangement.

When Louise had finished the telephone call, Alice walked over to the sink and said, "I think we should put this out where everyone can enjoy it."

She lifted the vase and spun around, holding it out in front of her, and nearly ran into Heather Ann Hammond.

"Oh!" Heather Ann took a step backward, already looking down at the water droplets that had sprayed her lavender-colored top.

Louise, who had settled into a chair not seconds earlier, leapt up and got a tea towel, which she offered the young woman.

"Oh, Heather Ann, I'm so sorry," Alice said. "I hope that won't leave spots on the fabric."

"It was my fault entirely. I didn't mean to sneak up on you." Heather Ann pinched at the soft drape of her sleeve. "Besides, there's no way a little water can hurt this fabric. I don't think you could spot this stuff with a laundry marker. It resists everything."

"Really?" Louise watched as Heather Ann dabbed at the water, which completely disappeared at the touch of the towel. "Ingenious."

"You bet it is. When you travel with Aunt Ida, you pack light and practical. You don't have the luxury of fussing over clothes that need ironing or dry cleaning. When you're trying to keep up with her, it's wash and wear, get up and go or get out of the way." Heather Ann extended her hand in a long, sweeping gesture.

"Then I take it your aunt has been more low-key on her visit with us than is her norm?" Louise asked, taking the towel from Heather Ann.

"Yes, much more low key."

"We hurdly saw her at all yesterday. I understood her needing her rest on Monday when she arrived, but I thought she'd be taking the town by storm yesterday."

"Me too. But she preferred to spend the day in, reading all the materials I'd gathered—back issues of the *Acorn Nutshell*, some pamphlets and so on. We did go for a rather long drive in the afternoon."

"Yes, I meant to ask if she had found everything she was looking for?" Louise asked.

"Yes, the family grave sites weren't exactly where she had thought, but most of the places she wanted to show me were just where she had promised they would be."

"She really is sharp," Alice said, touching her temple.

"Absolutely. But she says the car trip took more out of her than she expected, and also that it's colder here than she thought it would be." Heather

Ann glanced out the window and then at the breathtaking arrangement of flowers that Alice had set in the center of the kitchen table. "She said she thinks she has harbored such a warm and wonderful picture of Acorn Hill for so long that in her heart and mind it is always spring here."

"That's sweet, isn't it, Louise?"

"Not very realistic, but sweet," came the answer from the eldest sister.

"Or maybe she just wanted it to be spring, and she convinced herself it would be." Heather Ann slid her fingers along the curve of the lily. "To which I told her that she had gotten so used to ordering everything up to her specifications that she probably just thought the seasons would be no different."

Alice chuckled. "What did she say to that?"

Heather Ann's hand fell away from the flowers. Her shoulders rose and fell in a heavy sigh. "She said she wished she could have arranged for spring to greet her here because she didn't think she could wait until it actually arrived."

"The older I get the more I feel that way. Cold weather is not a friend to old joints and bones," Louise said.

"I got the feeling that she meant something else. She didn't say it outright. I have to tell you, we are not a demonstrative family. We don't burden one another with just any stray thought that pops into our heads. And we don't do that ourselves and we don't bear it graciously from one another. We are very private people."

Alice looked at Louise, not sure what to make of that claim after the welcoming gathering Ida Hammond had summoned.

"So it's just a feeling, really. But I think Aunt Ida feared that if she waited until spring had thoroughly taken hold, she might not have been well enough to travel or might not have been up to making a series of complicated decisions."

"Is your aunt ill, Heather Ann? Would you like me to check in on her?" Alice raised her head and listened for a moment, thinking she might hear a cough or movement that would indicate Ida Hammond was restless or in need of help. Alice nodded toward the tray. "I have everything ready for her medication. It would be no trouble for me to take it to her."

"Thank you. That's so thoughtful of you. I'll take them to her myself if you don't mind. She really prefers to have her mornings to herself. But before I do—"

The ringing phone interrupted them.

Louise shut her eyes for a moment and drew in a deep breath.

"Shall I answer that?" Alice asked.

"No." Louise held up her hand. "No. I think we should just let the answering machine pick up for now."

Alice looked puzzled, and even though she

didn't ask for an explanation, Louise supplied one. "That phone call earlier was from Carlene Moss. She wanted to pass along a warning."

"Warning?" Alice sat down across from Louise.

"Miss Moss from the newspaper?" Heather Ann's dark eyebrows slanted down and she stepped closer to Louise, her curiosity clearly piqued. "She promised to print my notice in today's edition. I hope there wasn't a problem."

"Not with the notice, no."

The phone stopped ringing and the answering machine clicked on.

Louise listened a moment, then relaxed and met Heather Ann's fretful gaze. "No, the notice was printed just as you asked. Carlene called to warn me to expect phone calls."

"Phone calls?" Alice settled back in her seat as the tension eased out of the moment. "Is that all?"

"But I specifically asked that no one call the inn or try to contact my aunt. I thought I made it clear that anyone who failed to respect her wishes would not be considered for an endowment."

"Yes. That was quite clear, and we certainly appreciate it." Louise folded her hands on top of the table. "But what Carlene called to tell me was that the story is being picked up in outlying areas, and she has already received some calls herself."

"I can't imagine it would be that big of a story." Alice adjusted the flowers on the table so that the sunlight sparkled over the crystal vase.

"Trust me, money is always news," Heather Ann said softly. "That's why I went to such lengths to spell out the circumstances under which it would be awarded."

"Carlene said it was only a couple of small-town reporters looking for a human-interest story. And beyond that, well, she did point out that when you put something like that in the paper, you should expect it to draw some attention. And not everyone will respect your wishes not to make contact."

"We'll just have to deal with the phone calls as they come. *If* they come," Alice proposed. "And in the meantime, you can take refuge in the parlor with your music students. I'll man the phone."

"Unfortunately, I don't have any students due today until midafternoon."

"Then you can go in there and use the time to do something else. What about your composition?"

"You write music?" Heather Ann put both hands on the back of one of the empty kitchen chairs, her face lit with interest.

"My sister is very talented," Alice chimed in.

"That's so fascinating. May I tell Aunt Ida? She loves music. In fact, she would love to offer support to at least one cause having to do with music."

"I haven't . . . that is . . ."

"I've always said that Louise should offer a course in music appreciation."

"You have? Since when?" Louise asked.

"Since I recalled how you helped me choose

some music to take for Lillian Dover to listen to in her last days."

Louise smiled and patted Alice's hand.

"Of course, we don't really have a place for that. The library would be too noisy and the churches already have so many activities going on."

"Plus, one would have to be sensitive to the feelings of the various music directors," Louise added.

"But someone of your caliber of achievement, Louise. With your experience, you have so much to offer." A single crease formed between Heather Ann's eyebrows. "I'll mention it to my aunt. Maybe she can think of something. She's surprisingly resourceful."

"Your aunt!" Alice gasped. "Her medicine. I'm surprised she hasn't come in here already wondering where it is."

"Well, actually, she went back to bed this morning. She had a restless night. And in truth, she isn't expecting her pills at the usual time."

"She isn't?" Alice asked.

"That's another little problem I have to discuss with you both. Only I don't want her to know I've come to you with it."

"Is your aunt all right?" Alice asked again, realizing she had not received an answer to that question.

"She's fine. For now."

Alice did not like the sound of that. She understood that this family guarded its privacy, but at a certain point evasiveness could cause difficulties.

"But you're *anticipating* a problem?" Louise asked, clearly agitated by Heather Ann's reluctance to say what was on her mind. "We can't be of much help unless you tell us what is going on."

"Yes, you're right. It's just that I know how embarrassing this will be for Aunt Ida. She so wants to make a positive lasting impression. I know she wouldn't want to seem to be—"

"Heather Ann, you know we are happy to help in any way that we can," Louise said in a firm but motherly tone.

Alice was a bit taken aback, but she suspected that her older sister knew exactly what she was doing.

Heather Ann nodded. "It's my aunt's medication. She put all her pills in a big pill box, one with a container for every day of the month."

"Yes," Alice said, "those can be very handy."

"If you fill it properly. But if you only fill some of the spaces, run out of medicine and leave the empty prescription bottle back home, dump other pills in a bottle you've had for years because it's smaller and doesn't have a childproof cap, then neglect to tell your lone traveling companion what you've done, those handy devices become a real nightmare." Heather Ann put her hand over her eyes and rubbed the bridge of her nose for a second. "She keeps telling me she has her own system. I wouldn't mind if her stubbornness and wanting to keep everything under wraps didn't make the problem so hard to resolve."

"What a mess," Alice murmured.

Heather Ann shook back her soft black hair and pressed on, saying, "In her defense, she has done things like this for a very long time. Always her way, always without informing a soul or feeling she owed anyone an accounting for her choices."

"Creatures of habit," Louise murmured. "Ned and I had a discussion about this the day he checked in. As we get older we tend to cling to our habits. We depend on them to make us feel safe and then when something comes along to upset the way we do things, we don't deal with it as quickly or as well as we did when we were young."

"That's her to a T. She's always done things her way and doesn't see why she should change. But when she rushed into taking this trip, everything sort of got off track." Heather Ann went to the tray and picked it up.

"Doesn't she carry her prescription information when she travels?" Alice asked. "People should never travel without all their medical information available to them at a glance."

Heather Ann gave a helpless shrug. "She gets her prescriptions filled at the largest chain drugstore in the country. With them we're never more than a few computer keystrokes away from all Aunt Ida's data."

"But you're in Acorn Hill now and we don't

have any big chain drugstores." Louise shook her head.

"You could drive over to Potterston," Alice suggested.

"Or," Louise raised one finger, "we could pay a visit to our very own Parker Drug and have a little chat with a certain pharmacist, who I am sure will be able to help."

"It's an awfully big imposition." Heather Ann set the tray aside with a quiet rattle and chewed her lower lip anxiously. "Do you think he'll mind?"

"Mind? No, of course not." Louise reached out and brushed the back of her fingers over the edges of the tulips, practically humming as she did. "In fact I am sure Ned will know just what to do, and it will do him a world of good to know we didn't hesitate to turn to him for help."

R-r-i-i-n-n-g.

Louise stood as if all had been settled. "I say let's follow Jane's lead and get out of the house this fine sunny morning. We can sort out this pill problem and it will get us away from that phone for a while."

Chapter Seven

*F**ormer Resident Seeks Worthy Beneficiaries.* Jane knew the *Acorn Nutshell* headline by heart. The newspaper had hardly hit the stands before people all over town were discussing the

89

big news. And with Mrs. Hammond staying under her roof, Jane seemed to the townsfolk the perfect source for information. It made her feel a bit like a celebrity, which made her feel guilty, because, well, she *liked* that feeling.

"Sorry, I really have no details. I only know what's in the paper," she told people who approached her with questions.

"Practicing to be a politician?" Sylvia Songer stood in the open doorway of her business, Sylvia's Buttons, grinning at her good friend.

"A politician?" Jane pulled up short, realizing she'd almost walked right by the place where she was headed.

"You have the distant smile, the vague response, the earnest look. Why, you're practically campaign-ready."

Jane laughed. "I see what you mean. I guess I got carried away trying to be polite but discreet."

"It would be pretty hard not to get carried away with the whole town buzzing about your guest." Sylvia was framed by the doorway and looked at one with her shop, an excellent advertisement for her dressmaking skills in her fashionable brown raw-silk dress. "Everyone I've met today has had his or her feet in the clouds," she said as she brushed back a strand of her strawberry-blond hair.

"Don't you mean had their heads in the clouds?"

"Do I?" she asked in a way that suggested she did not.

"Yes. I believe one has one's feet on the ground and/or one's head in the clouds."

"*Hmmm*." Sylvia tipped her head to one side, her gaze seeming to scan skyward as if she was trying to picture the very image. "I'm sure I've heard people say they are dancing on clouds."

"Oh, speaking of dancing, guess what I saw in Potterston yesterday?" Jane said.

"What were you doing in Potterston yesterday?"

"Meet me at the library after you close today, and I'll show you." Jane smiled to think of the decorations and how they would add just the right touch of fun and flair to her event.

Nia had loved her choices and hoped to keep some of the things in storage for future use—perhaps a unit on books made into movies. Of course it didn't hurt that this meeting of the book club, complete with appropriate decorations, cast the library in a favorable light while Mrs. Hammond was in town evaluating causes that served the community. Jane hoped that the movie club might help the library receive a nice grant. It would show that the building was well utilized, and in fact, that it could use some expansion of its meeting facilities.

"Come in and tell me all about this trip to Potterston," Sylvia said, motioning to Jane to enter.

"I'd love to." Jane started inside but Sylvia stopped her.

"First bid farewell to your constituents." Sylvia

laid a hand on Jane's shoulder and made a graceful gesture toward the sidewalks of Acorn Hill.

Happy to play along, Jane pivoted, raised her hand and gave a most politically correct wave. "I shall return," she called to the now empty street.

"After I have cranked her down a notch or two to get her head and her feet out of the clouds," Sylvia called out to no one just before she followed Jane inside the shop.

"It was very nice of Alice to stay with Aunt Ida while we came down to sort out this mess with her medicine." The brisk air gave the tip of Heather Ann's nose a healthy pink tinge. She cinched the belt of her pearl gray all-weather coat and raised her face into the early spring sunlight.

"It only made sense." Louise knew the short walk down the street to the pharmacy would invigorate them both. Being out on a day like this was just the thing to clear the mind, sharpen the senses. "Someone has to be there to explain things to your aunt when she wakes up and to monitor phone messages."

"I am so sorry to have brought all this extra work down on you all. I can assure you there'll be some extra compensation for it added to our payment."

"Oh no! We couldn't accept anything but our regular fee." Louise matched Heather Ann's long strides. "I know you've come to town to give away money, Heather Ann, but I think you'll find that the people in this town are not as interested in profiting from your aunt's visit as they are in knowing that her actions will benefit their friends and neighbors."

"But Aunt Ida and I have been such a bother to you and your sisters. Coming with me to the pharmacy is hardly a regular service."

"No, now don't worry about it. I'm really enjoying being out of the house in the fresh air."

"I guess I was naïve to think that Aunt Ida's eccentricities wouldn't spill over onto the people she was trying to help."

"She doesn't seem so eccentric to me."

"Well, how about set in her ways, then?"

"Self-assured," Louise countered.

"*Hmmm.* I have an idea." Heather Ann paused before crossing the street to the pharmacy. "Let's ask Alice what she'd call the indomitable Aunt Ida after tending to her for even a little while."

Louise laughed. "Alice will be just fine. She's cool-headed, kind-hearted and surprisingly quick on her feet."

"She'll have to be to keep up with Aunt Ida." Heather Ann's eyes twinkled with unexpressed laughter. "She has an iron will, you know."

"And Alice has nerves of steel."

"Iron and steel. That should definitely produce some sparks. Maybe we should pick up the pace and get this errand over with before they set the inn on fire."

• • •

"Are those flowers for me?" Ida used her cane to point to the arrangement resting on the kitchen table.

"No, ma'am. They were sent to me," Alice said, then realized that the older woman who had just appeared in the kitchen was carrying the empty silver tray under one arm and the water glass in the hand not holding the cane. She jumped up to take them from Ida and set them on the countertop.

"What's the occasion?" Ida asked.

"To be perfectly frank, I'm not sure."

The tall woman with the cottony white hair pulled up into a tight bun leaned forward, almost burying her face in the fragrant arrangement. "Tulips, iris, peonies and . . . ?"

"And a calla lily and some eucalyptus," Alice said. "The reason for their delivery has me in a quandary."

"Probably for me." Ida Hammond held both hands out to receive the vase.

The woman was so insistent that Alice took a step toward the vase to comply. "You are more than welcome to take them to your room to enjoy them, Mrs. Hammond, but truly the flowers were sent to me."

Ida pulled back with her chin tucked down. Her kindly expression soured and the folds of neck gave her the overall impression of a disapproving turkey about to raise a squawk. "And who are *you*?"

"I'm Alice Howard," she said gently. "I'm one of the sisters who owns this bed-and-breakfast where you and your niece—"

"No, dear, you misunderstand." She shook her head and waggled her cane in the exact same rhythm. "I haven't lost my senses. I'm just a tad out of whack."

"Out of whack?" Alice pulled out a chair and offered the seat to her guest with a wave of her open palm.

"Yes." Ida settled down, using her cane to help steady her descent. "As if, you know, I was going along my way and somebody came by and tapped my little trolley onto the next track. I can certainly make sense of everything. I'm just having to get used to viewing it from a different perspective."

Alice nodded. "I know that feeling."

"I know *who* you are. You are a nurse, your sister teaches piano, the other one cooks and your father was a minister. Passed away not too long ago."

"That's right."

"My condolences, dear."

"Thank you," Alice said. "But if you knew all that why did you ask me who I am?"

"The flowers." Ida tipped her head forward and in doing so showed that her hair was not pure white but streaked with faded gray.

Alice realized that Ida probably had once been as dark-haired as her grandniece. Dark-haired and tall and straight as a tree. And strong too, of body and spirit, Alice suspected. What an impressive figure she must have made. She still made.

"What about the flowers?" Alice asked.

"I wanted to know *who* you are that people would be sending you such an elaborate arrangement of flowers."

And not sending them to me, Alice mentally filled in Ida's unspoken message. Of course Mrs. Hammond thought there would be flowers and probably all sorts of messages and gifts waiting for her once people heard about her magnanimous plans. It made Alice wonder if she had even seen the notice in the newspaper that expressly discouraged any such attempts to curry favor. The Hammond family really did not communicate well at all. "Good question. A very good question indeed."

"It is an hour past the time I take my pills." Ida Hammond tapped the round gold watch that she wore on a long chain around her neck. "Where are those girls?"

A spontaneous smile touched Alice's lips. Not only had Ida referred to Louise as a girl, but the elderly woman's tone also implied that Louise was touched by the carefree attitude and irresponsibility that sometimes accompanied youth.

"My sister and your grandniece have gone to sort things out with the pharmacist at the drug store, Mrs. Hammond."

"Why did they have to go down there? Couldn't they just make a phone call?"

"They had to take all the information to Ned so they could get everything taken care of."

"Well, they didn't take everything."

"Oh? Did they overlook something important?"

"They overlooked me!" she declared. "And something else. I have a system. I know about my medicines and what the doctor told me regarding each and every one of them. If people are going to go to discuss my situation with a stranger, the least they could do is ask me to come along." She sounded more hurt than angry.

That touched Alice and she tried to smooth things out with a gentle tone and a sensible answer. "You were still asleep. I think they hoped to see to everything before you woke up."

"I'm not a child expecting a visit from St. Nick, you know." Her assertion might have carried more weight if she hadn't made such a pitiful and pouting face as she spoke. "I understand that medicine comes through doctors and pharmacists. I just think that if anyone would know how best to make sense of it all, it would be me."

Heather Ann thought differently, but Alice was not going to say that to the elderly woman. From her antique earrings to her chic black cashmere jacket and fetching red wool dress, Ida Hammond appeared ready to take on the whole town, not to mention her grandniece and unsuspecting, well-meaning Louise.

"How would you have felt if they had done this

97

to you?" Ida asked. "Went off without you to discuss your health issues with a total stranger?"

Alice hesitated but then admitted, "I wouldn't like it at all."

"Good. Then you won't mind taking me to this drug store so I can rectify the situation immediately."

Chapter Eight

As Louise held open the door to the drugstore for Heather Ann, she was struck by the importance of this store in her life. Her family had had many a prescription filled here and depended on the place for everyday needs, from cough drops to school supplies. Louise had selected and received many birthday cards from the store's overflowing racks. And the candy! If she could gather together again all the coins she'd slid across the counter as a child in the pursuit of jaw breakers, chocolate bars and lemon drops, she wouldn't be able to lift their weight.

"Isn't this quaint!" Heather Ann exclaimed as she followed Louise inside.

Louise let the door close behind them. The little bell, which had hung on the door for as long as she could remember, jangled to announce their entrance. "I suppose it *is* quaint, but it's so much more than that. It's like a time capsule of my childhood."

Louise's eye went to the old candy bins beside the front counter and she smiled, happy as always to see they had not changed in all these years. Yellow-wrapped pieces of molasses candy, big red cinnamon balls, wax lips, mustaches and false teeth, and packages of little wax bottles containing bright, sweet-tasting liquid filled the dark wood bins. On the counter were tall glass canisters that held peppermint sticks, strips of paper bearing tiny candy dots, licorice whips and a half dozen other old-fashioned treats.

As she moved down the aisle toward the back of the store, the wooden floor creaked familiarly. The wood's warm patina was worn in places by the footfalls of generations of Acorn Hill residents. It often occurred to her when in the store that her footsteps might be following the exact path that her mother and father once walked.

Only the soda fountain had changed, having been updated at least three times in the last sixty years to reflect the trends of the day. But more than the switch from wooden finishes to chrome and Formica to marble, what had changed the most were the prices. Louise glanced at the menu posted on the wall behind the counter and marveled that, when she was a teen coming here after a game, she could have a hamburger, fries and a chocolate malt for the same amount of money it now took to buy a single soda.

"I'm sure places like this are a real lifeline in a

small town like Acorn Hill." Heather Ann also had paused to take in the ambience of the store. "One of the things Aunt Ida had me research was Acorn Hill's access to health care. You hear so often how few doctors and providers can afford to stay in small towns and make a go of it."

"You did research on our town?" Louise asked in surprise.

"Statistics and demographic data and that kind of thing, mostly." Heather Ann's gaze continued to rove over the shelves and signs.

Louise could understand her interest. Parker Drug was a touchstone of Acorn Hill's past, through the warm and wonderful memories it evoked. Yet, it also was fully important in the present as a place where people often caught up with one another while shopping or waiting for a prescription. And, Louise thought, the store also represented the town's future. She looked around at all the medicines and treatments readily available here that would promise today's youngsters longer lives than their parents could expect.

"Hello, ladies." Ned walked from the platform in the back of the building to greet them.

"Well, look at you in your spiffy white lab coat and name badge, right out here with the customers." Heather Ann let her handbag slide from her shoulder, opened it and began gathering everything she had of her aunt's to give to Ned. "In those big chain stores I rarely see the pharmacists at all.

Well, maybe just the top of their heads while their assistants talk to me through a glass window or over a high counter."

"That's an advantage of Parker Drug over those chain stores," Louise said. "Here, the druggist can come right out and greet you if he isn't too busy. Chuck Parker does that all the time. He'll even walk around the store with you to help you locate things, and more than once he's run something over to us on his lunch break, so we wouldn't have to go out in bad weather."

"Sounds like he certainly earned this vacation of his," Heather Ann said as she transferred a piece of paper from one hand to the other and kept digging into the depths of her bag for more.

"I used to do those things." Ned shifted his shoulders, making the crisp cotton of his white lab coat rustle. "Before I sold my drugstores and made such drastic changes in my life."

He was longing for things to be the way they once were, Louise realized. Nostalgic for the familiar, a life that seemed less complicated because it existed only in his memory now. He was seeing things only as he wanted them to be, without the frustrations, failures or forgetfulness.

"Here you go." Heather Ann thrust everything she had collected into Ned's large, capable hands. "As I explained on the phone earlier, my aunt's medications are in a terrible mess. I hope you can make some sense of this all."

"That's my job," Ned said, trying to juggle the pillbox and the various pieces of paper on which Heather Ann had made notations and had jotted phone numbers from memory. "Do you want to wait while I go through this or shall I call you at the inn?"

"Oh, we want to wait," Heather Ann said emphatically before Louise could cast a vote about what they should do.

"I'll get working on it right away," Ned said. "Luckily, I got caught up on all the other orders I had just before you arrived." He turned and started back toward the pharmacy area.

"I don't even want to think about going back to Aunt Ida without her pills or at least an explanation and a plan for what we need to do next," Heather Ann said with an apologetic smile.

"I understand," Louise said.

A flash of color outside the store's windows caught Louise's attention. Her eyes widened and she shook her head. Then she touched the young woman's elbow and turned her so that she too could see out the window. Coming toward them were Sylvia Songer and Jane. The twosome was strolling cheerfully along the sidewalk, waving and bowing and calling out to people as they walked. *Sylvia must have closed the store for a coffee break*, Louise thought.

"Family relationships can be tricky," she said aloud with the lift of an eyebrow. "We love our kin, but sometimes we have to fight the urge to disown them entirely."

Heather Ann laughed merrily. "I know what you—" she began. Clearly something outside other than Jane and Sylvia's antics had upset her.

Louise looked in the direction that Heather Ann was staring just in time to see Ida Hammond approach the drugstore. The woman swept open the door with such force that the little bell actually flipped up over the top of the door on the small chain from which it dangled. She stood in the open doorway, pointed her cane at Louise and Heather Ann and cried, "Aha!"

"Am I crazy or did she just say aha?" Jane asked Sylvia from where they now stood in the doorway behind Alice and Mrs. Hammond.

"Yes," Sylvia said quietly and with a nervous giggle.

"Yes to which? Crazy or aha?" Jane frowned and went up on tiptoe to try to see into the store.

"*Shhh*," both Alice and Sylvia responded simultaneously.

The tip of Ida's cane came thumping down hard on the floor. "So this is where the pair of you went off to behind my back and right under my nose."

"Behind her back and under her nose? For an older woman she certainly is limber," Jane said, none too quietly.

Louise pressed her finger to her lips in a silent request that Jane rein in her commentary. She knew that her sister was trying to ease the tension between their guests, and in truth, it seemed that Mrs. Hammond was paying no mind to Jane's silliness, but Louise minded. "Jane, please," she finally said aloud, "this is between the Hammonds."

"Oh? Now it's between the Hammonds, but earlier when you conspired with my grandniece to sneak down here and usurp my independence with your meddling . . ."

"Sneak?" Louise homed in on the thing she found most insulting in the allegation.

"Meddling?" Alice repeated, mortified. A stickler for respecting the privacy of others, Alice was particularly upset by that accusation.

"Usurp?" Jane repeated in order not to be left out of the chorus of disbelief.

"Jane!" Sylvia, Alice and Louise all spoke sharply and at once.

Jane frowned. "I'm sorry, but there is no one else on earth who knows my sisters better than I, Mrs. Hammond, and I can attest that these things you have accused Louise of are simply not her style."

"Thank you, Jane," Louise murmured.

But Jane wasn't finished. "She's not a shrinking violet, no one would accuse her of that, but she is a good Christian woman who wants only the best for people. She doesn't stick her nose in where it doesn't belong. She doesn't sneak behind people's backs, and being an independent, accomplished woman in her own right, she would never do anything to usurp another person's free will."

Sylvia burst into applause, then realized what she had done, gasped and tucked her hands into the pockets of her hand-loomed rose-and-orange coat.

"I like her!" Ida stabbed one bony finger in Jane's direction.

"We are rather partial to her ourselves," said Louise with a wry smile. But much as her younger sister's loyalty and support warmed her heart, the cool air coming in from the open door had the opposite effect on her face and hands. "Now, why don't we all move out of the doorway and deal with this quietly and away from the chill?"

"Quite right." Ida took a few determined steps forward, creating enough room to allow the other women inside.

Jane went through the doorway after Alice and Sylvia, calmly giving the door a gentle shake after they passed through to dislodge the bell and its chain. Everyone who had grown up in Acorn Hill and had occasion to come flying through that door knew about dislodging the bell.

Jane paused a moment, feeling the blessing that, in this ever-changing world, some things remained the same.

"Do we really need all these people here to deal with Mrs. Hammond's prescriptions?" Louise asked when she saw how their party filled the front of the store.

"My point exactly!" Ida Hammond straightened

the beautiful black-and-red flowered shawl she had draped over her black jacket for warmth.

"I thought your point was that you believed we had interfered in your life and had gone sneaking off to do who knows what," Heather Ann said.

Ida threw one end of the shawl back over her shoulder. "Precisely."

Heather Ann shut her eyes. "And you wonder why I feel the need to oversee your affairs and keep tabs on your prescriptions."

"There. You said it again," Ida accused.

"What?" Heather Ann held her hands out, palms up.

"You acknowledged that they are my prescriptions." Ida dramatically pressed her hand to the center of her chest. "If anyone should be coming down to a drugstore to sort out *my* prescriptions, it should be me."

"Well, I must remind you that you took care of them to begin with," Heather Ann said to her aunt in a firm tone. "That's why you don't have them with you now and why *somebody* has to get them for you."

"And that *somebody* shall be me. I have been taking care of myself and my medical needs since before you were born, dear. When the time comes I can no longer do so, I assure you that I'll come to you and ask for your help."

Heather Ann rolled her eyes. A response that, luckily, her aunt did not see.

Louise fought the urge to speak. This was not her battle, and yet her mind was filled with recent incidents. There was her adult music student who needed help but didn't want anyone to know it. There was Ned, who was questioning his own competence because of two small memory lapses. And then there was Ida, who clearly needed assistance but was too proud to admit it. Louise sighed, but she kept her peace.

"Oh, Aunt Ida, you wear me out," Heather Ann finally said.

"See? There. You confess you're worn out and I tell you I'm not. I'm far from worn out yet. When that time comes I will ask for help." She gave a slow nod of her head in a movement so controlled that her meticulous little bun did not so much as tremble. "Until then I will remain in charge."

"And at full speed ahead, no doubt." Heather Ann put her hands on her hips. She shook her head, sending her dark hair dancing over her shoulders.

Ida did not respond to her grandniece but instead raised her cane in the air, giving it a shake, and called out, "Druggist! Druggist? I wish to see the druggist!"

For a few seconds no one spoke. The few other people in the store turned and looked and waited to see what would happen next in this odd little drama.

Finally Ned appeared at the end of the aisle, giving instructions to a customer he had been assisting. With a wave and a farewell, he clapped his hands together and strode confidently toward the cluster of women. When he came within a few feet, he stopped, smiled and rubbed his hands together. "Well, well. I have often observed that women go to the powder room in groups, but I didn't know that they also congregate in the powder *aisle* in the same way."

"The . . ." Alice looked around them, then started to laugh. She nudged Louise and pointed.

Sure enough, there they all stood, clogging up the passageway between shelves of squatty pink plastic and gold-and-white cardboard canisters marked in scrolled lettering "Rose-scented Talc," and big bold-colored containers proclaiming "helps fight athlete's foot" and "keeps feet fresh and dry all day."

"Ned," Louise said, stepping apart from the others, "Mrs. Hammond here—"

"Mrs. Hammond can speak for herself. Neither the cat nor old age has got her tongue." Ida stepped forward, and Louise nodded and stepped to the side to allow the older woman complete access to Ned.

"Tell me, what can I do for you?" Ned asked.

"It's about my pills," she said. "*My* pills. No one else's. The kind of thing I believe should be kept between myself and my health-care professionals, wouldn't you agree, Mr.—"

"Aunt Ida, this is Ned Arnold. Don't you

remember? He's in the room next door to yours."

"Oh, don't be silly. I do think I'd remember if a young man lived in the room next to mine! In fact, I've lived alone since I lost my Henry almost twenty years ago."

"Not in the room next to you at your house. At Grace Chapel Inn."

"Yes. Of course. Now I recall." Her face brightened. "You're the bellhop! You did an excellent job with my luggage, you know. Did I ever give you that tip I promised?"

"No, I couldn't accept anything. I'm actually a pharmacist."

Her smile quickly turned to a frown. "Then why do you moonlight as a bellhop? You must not be a very good druggist if you have to carry people's luggage to make ends meet."

"Oh, Aunt Ida." Heather Ann threw up her hands. "This is exactly the kind of thing that makes me think I need to oversee your—"

Louise put her hand on Heather Ann's and whispered, "Why don't we let Ned handle this? You can catch up with your aunt in a little bit."

"Carrying luggage for lovely ladies is not a sideline of mine, Mrs. Hammond." Ned took the woman's arm and threaded it over his as he began to lead her toward the back of the store. "I consider it a privilege."

"Oh? Oh, Mr. Arnold, how kind of you to say that." She said coyly, going along with him quite happily. "But you know you won't turn my head with flattery. I expect to see results on this pill problem . . ."

"I will do everything within my power to resolve the problem to your satisfaction, Mrs. Hammond." And they turned at the end of the aisle and disappeared.

"I wish I could be a fly on the wall back there so I could hear what my aunt is telling Mr. Arnold."

"You can trust Ned, Heather Ann," Louise assured her. "He'll take care of your aunt's health and her emotional well-being. He's not only a competent professional, he's also a very caring person."

The young woman nodded.

"He'll go over everything with her until he knows she has a grasp of all of his instructions," Louise said.

"And, of course, he'll send home written information detailing what the doctor prescribed and all the side effects and so on, so you'll have that to double-check on things," Alice added.

"Oh, I'm not worried about Ned in the least. He seems like a very kind and competent man. In fact, I wish we had someone like him back home."

"Now I wish that Ned were a fly on this wall, so he could have heard you say that."

"Why?" Jane asked.

"Is something wrong with Ned?" Alice chimed in.

"No. He just . . ." Louise couldn't divulge a confidence, especially one of the kind Ned had shared with her. "Let's just say that like everyone else, Ned deserves a lot more encouragement than he is accustomed to getting. It would be nice if he could hear the things people say about him. Knowing that people feel confident of his abilities and that they're positively affected by his attitude would certainly make his day."

Alice put her hand on Louise's shoulder. "You are a good friend, Louise, to think about that."

"Oh, it's no special talent to know when somebody needs his spirits lifted. We all could use it now and again. So often we go about our lives doing our best, giving our all, and we think that no one notices. Of course we don't do it for praise, and those of us with faith can count on the day when our work on earth is done and the Lord says, 'Well done, good and faithful servant.'" Louise took a deep breath and let it out slowly. "But it certainly would be nice if people could hear well-deserved praise before that time."

"My sister, gifted musician and closet philosopher." Jane held up her hand the way a magician's assistant might do at the end of a trick.

"It's a wonderful thought, Louise." Sylvia said softly. "And it is something that we can all do so easily, if we just think about it."

"Absolutely," Jane agreed. "In fact, I think you should give a little speech including that idea when we host the testimonial dinner for Mrs. Hammond."

"Testimonial dinner? I thought you were just going to gather a few people to acknowledge her and allow her to honor her family? Now it's a testimonial?" Louise could feel the wrinkles in her forehead deepening as she tried to grasp what her sister might be concocting.

"That's our Jane," Sylvia said. "Give her an inch and she'll throw a testimonial."

"Thank you. I think."

Heather Ann clearly had reservations about the idea. "It's a very lovely thought, Jane, but I think that a big celebration like that might be too much for—"

"Then do it, man! It's an excellent idea. Let's get cracking. Not a moment to waste!" Ida Hammond issued the orders to Ned, and though they were out of sight, everyone heard the emphatic thumping of the cane on the floor and knew that the woman had gotten a satisfactory result.

Heather Ann chuckled, lowered her head and shook it. "Okay, tell me more about this dinner idea of yours, Jane. A testimonial might not be appropriate, though, since no one here knows her well enough to speak about her."

"Fine." Jane slipped between Louise and Alice to take Heather Ann by the arm, turn her around and started walking her toward the door. "A dinner then. An appreciation dinner."

"Assuming there will be enough people eager to

show my aunt appreciation. Frankly, there simply may not be that many gifts given out, depending on what she decides."

"That just shows you how little you know about the people of your aunt's old hometown," Jane said. "They can appreciate the effort your aunt is making and celebrate the good fortune of their neighbors, even if their own causes never see a dime."

"You think so?"

"I know so. In fact, why don't you come out and about with Sylvia and me and meet with some folks to see how much your aunt's coming here has energized people?"

"Really?"

"Why not?" Sylvia gave a nod. "You should see firsthand how it's made them think about what can be done to improve things for most people here in Acorn Hill, about what a single person can do to make a difference."

A smile lit Heather Ann's face. "I am so happy to hear that. And I can't wait to see it for myself. This is a way I can be helpful to Aunt Ida without stepping on her toes."

"That's a wonderful idea, Heather Ann," Louise said. "Alice and I will stay behind and see that your aunt gets back to the inn safely."

"Thank you." And with that, Heather Ann, Jane and Sylvia went out the door, chattering and gesturing all at once.

The bell over the door had hardly settled into silence when Ned came down the aisle again.

"Oh." He watched as the three women made a left and headed down the sidewalk. "I just came to tell Miss Hammond what happened with her aunt's prescriptions. With Mrs. Hammond's permission, of course."

"Of course." Alice nodded. "But I'm afraid Heather Ann is off exercising her own independence."

"And doing a bit of research on Acorn Hill, putting names with places and people." Louise glanced toward the back of the building. "Where is your customer?"

"After I spoke with her doctor over the phone and confirmed her prescriptions, I was able to give her today's dosage. I gave her the pills and settled her into a chair in the waiting area, but she insists on having bottled water to take them."

"I'll get it for her," Alice volunteered. "I know just which brand she prefers." And off she went to the cooler near the cash register to take care of it.

"Good job, Ned. I knew if we brought this situation to you, you'd know just what to do."

"Well, it is my job."

"Still, Heather Ann wasn't sure anyone who didn't work in one of those large chain drugstores with the national network of computers could be of any help at all."

"Did you tell her we aren't completely without

resources here in Acorn Hill?" He laughed. "Actually I solved it using another one of those advances in phone technology that you and I marveled at having to learn in our lifetime."

"What's that?" Louise cocked her head.

"The fax machine."

"Oh, of course! A fax machine would get you the doctor's orders in a matter of minutes. Problem solved."

"In a matter of minutes after the doctor sends it. It may be later today before I can actually fill her prescription, but I told her I'd bring it to the inn when I return tonight."

"That's very thoughtful of you."

"Again, it's just my job. When I ran my own pharmacy I used to do deliveries on my way home all the time."

Louise supposed if she commented on that they could easily fall into another one of those nostalgic "those were the days" conversations. But why dwell on the past? Instead, she wanted to give Ned a chance to savor his success in helping Mrs. Hammond. "So, they had no problem with writing a new prescription for Mrs. Hammond?"

"Not under these circumstances. His nurse promised to get it out as soon as possible but she said they were rather overrun by a rash of patients with respiratory issues."

As if to prove the validity of that statement, a woman came in with a tissue pressed to her red-

115

dened nose. She sniffled, blinked her bloodshot eyes and mumbled something about needing relief in the form of a specific brand of decongestant.

Ned pointed to the next aisle over and told her that if she needed further help he was right there for her. Then he looked at Louise again. "We always see a lot of those this time of year, when it's still chilly enough for colds and just warm enough for the first signs of allergies."

"Where's my water? You can't be getting me water and gabbing with your friends at the same time, young man." Ida came toward them from the opposite direction of the woman with the sniffles. Her sturdy black shoes squeaked on the gray-and-white flecked floor. That seemed only to add to the air of impatience when she said, "I'm behind my time for my medicines and—"

"Here you go, Mrs. Hammond. I've got your water for you." Alice held aloft the bottle with the blue label and white plastic cap.

"Very thoughtful of you, dear." She shot Ned a thorny look as she went past him to meet Alice a few feet away. "I suppose one can't expect a glass under these circumstances."

"I guess I won't be getting a tip after all," Ned whispered to Louise, giving her a wink.

"Maybe when they leave you can carry their luggage to the car and she'll make up for it then," Louise suggested with a laugh. She felt real delight in seeing the obvious boost in Ned's self-esteem.

"Maybe so," he said. "But I think they may out-stay me. I'm only here for the three weeks that Chuck Parker is on vacation. How long do they intend to stay, do you know?"

Ahh . . . ahh . . . ahh . . . choo! The sneeze came from the woman in the cold-medicine aisle.

"That's it. I'm leaving." Ida headed for the door as fast as her bent legs and wavering gait could take her. "Don't forget my medicine, young man!"

She waggled her cane as her only form of good-bye and yanked the door hard enough to send the bell up over the top once again and out she went.

Alice looked at the open bottle in her hand, then at Louise and Ned, then at Ida who was making her getaway, and she sprang into action. Even after stopping to free the bell and let the door close quietly, she moved fast enough to catch up with the geriatric germophobe before she reached the corner, and she did this without spilling a drop of water.

"Alice must be a wonderful nurse," Ned commented as they stood and watched the two women make their way back toward the inn.

"One of the best in her field, according to those who know," Louise said. She wondered if she had told her sister recently how highly she and others thought of her work. "And she's in good company here. I think you are one of the best pharmacists we've ever had. Chuck Parker wouldn't have gone off for so long and left everything in your care unless he thought so too."

"It wasn't anything extraordinary, Louise. Just doing my job."

"And I'm just saying that you do it well. Can you accept that?"

"I can. I can also thank you very much. I know you will appreciate it when I say I'll never forget your kindness through all of this."

Chapter Nine

"Jane, I have to hand it to you, that really did put the spring back in my steps." Sylvia did a semi-twirl with the cardboard movie figure before putting it away in the library's storage room after the conclusion of the movie.

"The meeting of the movie club was a fun way to spend a Saturday afternoon," Nia said. She pointed the way for Sylvia, indicating where she should place the cutout next to the posters and other things they had taken down. She liked the decorations Jane had secured. She felt that she could use them again, which meant keeping them safe from curious little hands. "I was amazed that we had such a nice turnout and that people were so willing to participate in the discussion."

Jane popped the DVD into its case and snapped it shut. Though not exactly as she had envisioned it, the event had been a happy success if not a huge one. "I just wish Alice could have been here. She could have used the diversion like the rest of us."

"She did promise to substitute for her co-worker at a moment's notice," Louise reminded Jane. At the request of Heather Ann, Louise had divided her time between the movies and discussion and manning a table where guests could fill out survey forms about improvements they would like to see in Acorn Hill. While the others were removing the movie decorations, she gathered a handful of pencils from the survey table and snapped a rubber band around them. "One can't always make plans when babies are concerned. Babies have a way of making their own plans."

"I know, but I picked one of Alice's favorite movies just for her." Jane waved the slender DVD case under her chin like a hand fan and sighed. Because they didn't have a DVD player at the inn, she wondered if she and Alice could watch it at Sylvia's house later.

"Maybe the next time we do something like this Alice will be able to make it," Nia said.

"So you're willing to do it again?" Jane asked with some surprise in her voice. She'd been so focused on everything being over that she hadn't given much thought to what might come next. "I was worried that you might consider the movie club too much of a strain on the facilities."

"I'd rather try new things like this here at the library, strain or not, than not have them at all."

119

Nia went to the table where Louise was finishing up with the surveys and glanced down at a few of them. "While many people didn't stay for the whole meeting, more than a few told me they liked coming in and watching a bit of a movie or listening to part of a discussion while they waited for their kids to pick out books or filled out their surveys."

"I think it's quite telling how many people came by just to take this survey," Louise said, tapping the edge of a stack of papers on a table to tidy them. "This is such a wonderful community. People want to participate in making it even better and keeping it vital. We certainly owe Ida Hammond thanks, not only for what she is offering to do for us, but also for reminding us of what we already have."

"I'm still trying to pull things together for a dinner," Jane said. She dropped into a chair next to her sister and stretched out her legs. "But I'm not having any luck finding anyone who remembers the Lawson family."

Sylvia tucked away the last of the decorations, then came to join them. "Have you asked Ethel?"

Louise and Jane exchanged wide-eyed looks of near panic.

"Ask Aunt Ethel if she remembers someone who left town around seventy years ago?" Jane rolled her eyes. "Heaven help us!"

"In addition to the danger of asking such a question, Aunt Ethel moved to Acorn Hill twenty-some years after Ida left."

"I didn't mean asking her as if she remembered them personally. Surely, if the Lawson family was as influential as Heather Ann says they were, Ethel must have heard talk about them even years after they left. People around here tend to have long memories, especially when talking about the good old days," Sylvia observed.

"Just tell Ethel that of all the people in town who might have that kind of very useful information, you thought of her first. Play it up," Nia suggested. "Ask for her help."

"Not a bad idea," Louise murmured.

"True. Aunt Ethel does love to help." Jane made little quotation marks in the air with her fingers as she said the word *help*.

Everyone smiled knowingly.

She sat up a little straighter. "I think I will ask her."

"Wait until she's over her cold," Louise warned.

"Oh, good idea. If Ida Hammond found out I'd been associating with a person who had a raised temperature, she might check out of the inn and head for the hills."

"What hills?" Sylvia asked, prodding Jane's shoulder.

"Well, there are sure to be molehills that Aunt Ethel will turn into mountains," Jane said. "Particularly if she thinks we're trying to wrangle her age out of her in the guise of planning Ida Hammond's appreciation dinner."

"We'll figure something out, even if Aunt Ethel can't help us," Louise reassured her sister. She stood and stretched a bit as she surveyed the room to make sure that it looked as tidy as when they had arrived.

"All right, ladies, if we can find a place out of public view, I have a little treat for all of us," Jane announced, pulling out a basket that she had stowed behind the checkout desk.

Nia suggested that they use a table in the room that once had held row upon row of archived periodicals, which were now stored on microfiche and computer disks. There they shared a cup of tea and a plate of Jane's butterscotch brownies while they went over the surveys. Afterward, they would give them to Heather Ann for her aunt's perusal.

"Those old movie stars had so much style, such elegance, didn't they?" Jane sat with her elbows on top of the pile of surveys she was supposed to be reading.

"And such talent. It seems that they all knew how to sing, dance *and* act." Sylvia flipped through her stack of surveys, sorting out the ones with comments from ones that simply had preferences checkmarked. "Not many people have that kind of drive and dedication these days."

"Oh, I don't know," Jane said. "Think about the

stars in *Chicago*. They all learned to dance and sing as well as act for that movie. And they all did a great job." Jane proceeded to get up and do an imitation tap dance, while singing a few bars of "All That Jazz"—off-key, of course.

"Stop," Louise pleaded. "The next thing you know Jane's going to announce that she's going to take dancing and singing lessons so that she can run off to Hollywood and become a star."

Jane narrowed her eyes at her sister. "Maybe I won't run off to Hollywood, but I might get as far as Potterston."

"Potterston?" Sylvia asked.

"What are you thinking about doing, Jane?" Louise eyed her sister warily.

"Whatever it is, she has that look on her face that means trouble," Sylvia said with a laugh—and a look of interest.

"The first time I mention feeling up to strolling to a few spots around town, you walk a layer of rubber off the soles of my shoes!" Ida Hammond said. She lowered herself onto a wrought-iron bench that had been conveniently placed outside a quaint white building with a red roof.

Heather Ann joined her on the bench. "Oh, Aunt Ida, such an exaggeration!"

"No, I do believe my cane was an eighth of an inch longer when we left the inn for the library earlier today." She squinted one eye at the tip. "But the fresh air and friendly exchanges have done me good, I must admit."

"It really is a lovely little town, isn't it?"

"I always thought so, even as a child. Coming back here has only confirmed my deep-seated belief that so much of what I have accomplished in life began here in Acorn Hill. From little acorns mighty oak trees grow."

"I suppose if I were the kind of niece who liked to rib her dear old aunt, I might ask if that means that even a little nut can make something big of itself if it has good roots."

Ida laughed.

"So, where to next? Are you ready to go back to the inn?"

"Let's see, where have we visited so far this fine, warm afternoon?"

"The General Store, the Coffee Shop."

"And you made notes on what everyone said there, right?"

Heather Ann whipped out her green leather appointment book and flipped to the last pages under the header "notes."

"June Carter, at the Coffee Shop, suggested we do something for the ANGELs because they play such a positive role in the community."

"Oh, I liked her. Up-front and honest. When I commented on how good the muffins looked, she came right out and said they came from the . . . the . . ."

"The Good Apple Bakery."

"That's the place. Did we go there?"

"No. But we can if you like."

"Maybe Monday. I don't think I have much walking left in me today. What else have you got written down there?"

"At the General Store, we ran into Carlene Moss. You remember her from the *Acorn Nutshell*?"

"Yes. I hope she understood why doing another article in the paper asking for suggestions would come too late."

"I'm sure she did. Otherwise no one else had any concrete ideas about your donation, just assurances that whatever way you found to invest in Acorn Hill would be fruitful and appreciated."

"I truly believe that now, not that I really doubted it before, but it does one's heart good to hear your beliefs are justified now and again. Is that all you have noted?"

"I made note of all the people we've met. Then, we have the library, of course, and the input from the surveys they are doing there." Heather Ann raised her head to scan their surroundings. "I hope Jane's movie gathering went well."

"I hope they *gathered* plenty of those surveys. I intend to spend a good deal of time tomorrow going over those."

"You spend so much time in your room, Aunt Ida. The ladies might think you don't like them."

"Oh, I like them fine. They really are quite interesting, you know. Besides, I'm not always in my room. I move from place to place at the inn. Sticking close has its advantages. I hear a lot of what goes on there, what the sisters are up to and so on."

"Aunt Ida! You don't mean you've been eavesdropping?"

"Of course not! It's just that while moving about the inn, one picks up things. They talk in the hallways and as I pass by rooms. I'm not talking about anything that anyone is trying to keep a secret, just the bits and bobs of everyday life."

"And you find that interesting?"

"Oh yes. I lead a very ordered life you know, dear. Dedicated so much of my time to work and managing the family finances. I find myself quite fascinated by the everyday doings of Grace Chapel Inn. The Howard sisters really are lovely, cheerful people."

"Yes they are. Just like so many people here in town."

"Perhaps we should meet some more of them, then." Ida planted her cane on the sidewalk and, steadying herself with it, glanced over her shoulder. "Where are we now? What is this place?"

"Nine Lives Bookstore. Viola Reed, owner," Heather Ann read the neat gold lettering on the door.

"A bookstore! I bet this Viola Reed has quite a bit of information on the locals and probably an opinion or two on community needs as well!"

"Let's go in and find out, shall we?" Heather Ann stood and offered her arm to her aunt.

Louise had arranged the surveys into stacks, put them into file folders and taken them back to the inn's library, where she thought Heather Ann and Ida could review them in comfort and in private.

Jane and Sylvia also came back to the inn, where they made their way into the parlor to listen to some CDs that they claimed might inspire them in their new endeavor: salsa dancing!

Louise shook her head at the very notion: fifty years old and suddenly deciding to take up salsa dancing. Louise wondered if she would ever understand her youngest sister.

"How could Jane and Alice and I have turned out so differently?" she asked softly of no one. Or perhaps she was speaking to someone. She glanced around the library with its deep, rich colors of green and rust and gold. With the reminders of Daniel Howard in the photos, his pen collection and other things that he had cherished in his marriage to her mother, Louise did not have to look far to find her father here. She took a deep breath.

Enough time had gone by since her father's death that Louise no longer felt the sense of loss and loneliness over her father's passing. She could, instead, think of him with real joy in her heart. He had lived a good, distinguished and remarkable life. He had given his full measure, and she knew that when he had stood before the Lord at last he had heard those words she had quoted in the drugstore: "Well done, good and faithful servant."

It was impossible to look around this room and not be reminded of all her father had accomplished, and of all the twists and turns he had faced, and to note that through good times and bad he had found the gifts of a youthful spirit and a mature faith. He had never feared what each new day would bring.

And in those thoughts Louise had the answer to her question. She and Alice and Jane were not really so different. They were the people their father had raised them to be—themselves, individuals who held the values Daniel Howard had instilled in them.

"Well, maybe salsa dancing isn't such a bad idea," she muttered as she moved toward the door. She reached into her pocket and withdrew the lace hankie that she kept there, dabbing the dampness from her eyes. She raised her eyes and smiled. She turned, thinking she might go up to her room to do some Bible reading in preparation for church the next day. As she was about to flip off the light switch, the sound of the front door opening and closing startled her.

She glanced at her watch. Seven o'clock. Alice would only now be finishing up the shift she had worked for her friend. Heather Ann and Ida

Hammond were having dinner with Lloyd Tynan, discussing his vision of what was most needed in the town. Louise turned off the lights and went to see who had come through the front door.

"Oh, hello, Louise." Ned Arnold stood just inside the door and slipped out of his tan trench coat. He looked tired.

"Isn't it a bit late for you to be coming home on a Saturday? Chuck usually closes by six."

He nodded. "I locked the doors and turned over the Sorry We're Closed sign right on time, but I was delayed because of Mrs. Hammond's pills."

"Oh, I'm so sorry that you are still working on that problem. I thought you got that all sorted out days ago."

"Well, it turns out she only told me about the pills that she had run out of on that day. I found out today that she took the last of what she calls her heart pills. She asked me this morning to take care of it for her."

"Oh dear." Louise shut her eyes. Mrs. Hammond was really a sweet old soul, but Louise did not like the idea of her ordering about other guests. "Did that pose a problem for you?"

"No, actually it was no trouble at all."

"Her doctor was in his office and willing to fax you the prescription?"

"Oh, I didn't need a prescription."

"Didn't need a prescription for heart medication?" Louise asked.

"If you recall, I said she 'calls' them her heart pills." Ned smiled slyly. "And I suppose her doctor told her when he put her on the regimen that they were to keep her heart healthy."

"May I ask what they are? Vitamins? Calcium? Indigestion tablets?"

"Baby aspirin." He held up a small white bag with neatly typed information stapled to it.

"Baby aspirin?"

"She takes one every day with her regular medicines, probably along with a few of those other things you mentioned. It's a very common recommendation." He smiled. "So common it's easy to forget about entirely."

Louise put her hands to her cheeks, and asked with a rueful laugh, "Oh no, Ned. You *didn't*?"

"Oh yes, I did," he said, rolling his eyes upward. "Went right off and forgot all about them."

"Oh, Ned, but it isn't as if it's a life-or-death medication. You were just doing a favor that was asked of you when your mind was focused on getting home. We've all done something like that."

"That's what I keep telling myself. That it's the kind of forgetfulness we all experience." He shook the bag, and the pills rattled.

Louise had the impression the man wished he could give himself a shake as well for his perfectly normal memory lapse.

"Anyway," he said, sounding just a bit more at

peace with the whole thing. "I made it all the way back to the inn after closing up the store. I bounded onto the front porch and was within an inch of placing my hand on the doorknob when it struck me."

"Oh no."

"Oh yes. It struck me that if I walked through that door without these pills, Mrs. Hammond might just whack me."

"Oh, Ned," Louise said, laughing.

"Might just take her cane to me and chase me all the way back down to retrieve her precious heart pills." He raised his hand as if he were grasping the all-too-familiar walking stick and gave it an outraged jiggle just as Mrs. Hammond might have done.

"That would have caused quite a stir in town."

"I ran back to get the pills and here I am."

"I hope you didn't actually run all the way back," she said.

"Let's say I walked as fast as I could without causing alarm in people who saw me." He ran his hand back through his silver hair. He kept it so neat and short that the gesture did not leave a ruffle or a wake. "I unlocked the door and slipped inside without turning on the lights. I was able to get the aspirin easily because I had left the package on the counter by the cash register. I got the pills, shut the door—maybe a little harder than necessary because I was so disgusted with myself—then I flipped the lock and hurried back here, hoping no one would be the wiser."

"I guess I foiled your plans."

"I should have seen it coming, Louise. No one is wiser than you."

"I wouldn't say that," she said.

"Of course you wouldn't, because you are far too wise to heap praise on yourself. That's what you have friends for." He handed her the bag, gave a nod and headed up to his room.

"Mayor Tynan, you really didn't have to go to this much trouble for us," Heather Ann whispered as they sat in Zachary's supper club, Acorn Hill's finest eatery.

"No trouble, Miss Hammond. I know how your aunt feels about . . . her privacy." Lloyd Tynan gave Ida Hammond a sharp salute.

She acknowledged the gesture with an indulgent smile.

"Yes, but asking them to move our table away from everyone else's?" Heather Ann extended her hand to indicate the waiter in his black pants and tie who had discreetly shown them to a table near the back of the restaurant. "We really never intended to cause such a stir."

"Speak for yourself, Heather Ann." Ida leaned her cane against the edge of the table and threw back her shoulders. In her charcoal-gray suit, high-necked ecru lace blouse and brilliant blue silk scarf that she wore over one shoulder, she was the image of a queen surveying her realm. Except, of course, a true royal might not have opted for the silver-trimmed running shoes Ida had chosen for the evening. "While I certainly wanted to make this gift to Acorn Hill to reward the town that gave me my start, I don't mind receiving a little bit of attention for it. After all, I won't be here forever."

"Of course, Aunt Ida," Heather Ann said softly. She lowered her gaze and her expression grew somber.

Lloyd cleared his throat. "Yes, well, everyone likes a little special consideration now and again, don't they? And we're happy to provide."

"Thank you." Ida tipped her head in gracious acceptance. "I only hope you realize that I do not expect special treatment because I am rich or old or because I plan to give away a large sum of money."

Lloyd struggled to find the appropriate answer to that. "Oh . . . of course not . . ."

Ida let him off the hook. "I expect special treatment because this is Acorn Hill and that's how people behave here. No matter who you are or what you may or may not have to offer them, the people of this town treat you as if you are special."

"Exactly!" Lloyd reached out as if he wanted to give Ida's arm a squeeze, caught himself, then tapped his hand lightly on the table for emphasis instead. "Exactly."

"Don't let her fool you," Heather Ann said as she stood. "She expects special treatment wherever she goes."

"That's why she brings her lovely niece along wherever she goes," Lloyd said with confidence.

Heather Ann accepted the compliment with a smile, then excused herself to go wash her hands before the meal arrived. She made a lovely figure, illuminated by the glow of the candles on the tables, walking gracefully across the wine-colored carpet in her beautifully draped teal silk dress.

"So, Mrs. Hammond," Lloyd began once they were alone, "How are you finding our charming town?"

"How am I *finding* it? Don't you really want to know how I will be funding it?"

"No, honestly, I only want to ensure that your stay here is pleasant."

"You and I are not young and coy, Mayor Tynan. Let's speak frankly. While I'm sure that you are most sincere in your well wishes, I know that you must also be quite curious about my plans."

"Well, it is rather exciting. Have you come to any conclusions?"

"I've looked over the surveys that were taken at the library. I've driven around town. I've met with the mayor—quite a handsome and congenial fellow."

Lloyd bowed slightly.

"And I have a few ideas. There are a handful of

things that I think need doing here in Acorn Hill, but then that's the problem, isn't it?"

"What?"

"I don't live in this town."

"Oh."

"Things change. Even Acorn Hill has changed since I lived here, though not in substantial ways, but to my eyes." She smoothed the palm of her hand down the brushed steel arm of her chair. "The needs I expected to find in the Acorn Hill I carry in my memory are not the needs of the real place."

"I can well imagine."

"I'm going to have to give this all a lot of thought."

"And I know that you will come to the right conclusion," he said without hesitation.

"Thank you." She reached out and patted his arm. "You are one of a very few people in recent years to express that kind of conviction about my abilities."

Lloyd glanced down at her hand still on the sleeve of his suit jacket.

Her eyes followed his line of vision.

"Oh." She laughed and patted his arm again. "Oh, that, that not-shaking-hands-and-so-forth business?"

"We all thought you had an aversion to . . ."

"To human contact? No, not at all. Human germs I can do without, but touch? It's vital to one's health and well-being."

"Then why the . . ." He demonstrated the salute she had suggested they use.

"Because it's smart. Because it's safe. Because . . ." She glanced around to make sure her niece wasn't approaching, then leaned in to whisper, "Because I have plans for late spring and early summer and I do not want them spoiled by a common cold."

"Plans?"

She leaned in even more and lowered her voice once again. "As soon as I've made my decision here, I plan to scoot on out of Acorn Hill and straight to the nearest seaport and book an ocean cruise."

"A cruise?"

"Nothing too taxing. I've spent most of my life running the family business. Keeping to a schedule. Overseeing other people's problems. I hear on these cruises they cater to your every whim. I think I deserve a little catering, don't you?"

"Absolutely."

"People like to go around saying 'you're only young once,' but let me tell you, Mayor Tynan, I'd rather people realize that you only *live* once. I may not be young anymore, but I am still alive, and I intend to live it up."

"That's wonderful, Mrs. Hammond. A cruise. You will enjoy that."

"Yes. I haven't told Heather Ann about it yet because she worries."

"I can . . . just imagine," was all Lloyd could manage to say before the young woman rejoined them and they all settled in for a lovely meal.

They ate and chatted about the places Ida had visited, never once straying to talk of her plans either for the cruise or her money.

"Mayor Tynan, I have to say that I never expected to be served such a wonderful meal in such a small town." Heather Ann said as she nodded to the waiter who placed a slice of dark-chocolate cake in front of her. "In fact, it's all been so good that I hardly have room for this dessert."

"Take a tip from someone older and more experienced, my dear." Ida took a moment to appreciate the aroma and appearance of the lemon mousse she had ordered. "Life is short. You should always leave room for dessert."

"You are a very wise woman, Mrs. Hammond. Myself, I have always tried to do that very thing. Except I often eat too much, but have the dessert anyway." Lloyd patted his round tummy. "As you might have guessed looking at me."

Ida, politely, did not look. Instead she took a bite and savored it. And in response to the delicious tart-but-sweet taste and delicate texture, she could only think to suggest, "Maybe you should skip the meal and go straight for the dessert then, Mayor Tynan."

"A very wise woman indeed," Lloyd said, laughing. "But as you were saying, Heather Ann, people are often quite pleasantly surprised to find out how well we eat here in Acorn Hill. The baked goods, the new exotic foods stocked at the General Store, the fine dining here at Zachary's and, of course, the unsurpassed culinary delights prepared by Jane Howard at Grace Chapel Inn."

"It was very kind of her to offer to provide most of our meals instead of just breakfast. Her meals have been among the best I've ever had," Ida chimed in with a nod.

"And that's saying something. Aunt Ida has dined in some of the best eating places in the world."

"I think it's the setting." Ida took another bite. "Oh, Jane's food is without rival, yes, but you cannot discount atmosphere. There is no better complement to a meal than the feeling of being nestled in a sweet, secure spot full of good, caring people."

"So true," Lloyd said.

"I'll definitely miss the town *and* Jane's cooking when we leave. Won't you, Aunt Ida?"

"So much that I think we may have to come back again some time to sample both. And *this*." She took another bite of her mousse.

"We'd love to have you back in Acorn Hill any time, Mrs. Hammond. And you, as well, Heather Ann."

"We'd love to return," Heather Ann said.

"But just in case we can't do that in a timely

fashion, I wonder if they would provide the recipe for this lovely mousse for me to give to my cook? I'd gladly pay for it."

"I can't speak for the restaurant, Mrs. Hammond, but I have a feeling we can work something out."

"Won't influence my decision, of course. That wouldn't be fair."

"I'm sure no one in Acorn Hill expects you to be anything but fair, Mrs. Hammond." He gave her arm a pat, then leaned in to give her a wink even as he called the waiter over to their table. "And well fed!"

After the meal, the affable mayor offered to take the women for a drive to show them the town by moonlight, but Ida was ready to head back to the inn. She had had a fruitful but tiring day. She wanted to get her rest so she could be sharp for church the next morning and for the task ahead of her, reading the surveys and considering how this special town would most benefit from her gift.

Alice came home tired from her substitute shift, and after some time with Jane and Sylvia, stopped by Louise's room to say good night.

"You look done in." Louise said. She had been sitting up in bed with her Bible. "Hard shift?"

"Actually, it was a bit more tiring than usual." Alice checked out her reflection in Louise's dresser mirror. She blew out a long breath in a nearly silent whistle, then ran her fingers through her short bob in an attempt to tidy her hair. "I've been chatting with Jane and Sylvia about the movie club."

"Jane was disappointed you weren't there to participate. It actually went very well."

"Yes, she told me all about it and she seemed very pleased. She also told me about her plans to take up salsa dancing."

"Are you going to join her in that?" Louise asked, a faint smile on her lips.

"I will if you will!" Alice gave a wiggle with a little Latin flare.

Louise chortled. "Good night, Alice," she said.

"Good night, Louise. Sleep tight."

"I plan on it," she called back, placing her bookmark between two pages of the sixth chapter of Matthew, then setting her Bible aside. Louise suspected the entire household would sleep especially well after this demanding day.

Chapter Ten

The telephone rang, jarring Louise awake in the middle of the night. For a few seconds she wasn't sure where the noise came from or what had made it. But when it sent its shrill scream through the silent house a second time, she threw back the covers, grabbed her robe and hurried to answer it, her heart pumping.

On her way to the table in the upstairs hallway

where the phone was located, she accounted for the members of the household. Alice had made it home from work safely. Ned too. Jane had spent the evening in. And Louise had heard Heather Ann and Ida Hammond return from dinner with Lloyd shortly before nine. All were safe and sound. She could happily dismiss the idea of an accident. Then her mind went to Aunt Ethel. She had been ill and, while each of the sisters had taken turns going over to her house daily, no one had looked in on her this evening. Her conscience chafed her. *Aunt Ethel only has a cold*, she argued with her inner voice. *Colds turn into other things like pneumonia*, the voice argued.

R-r-r-i-i-i-n-n-g!

Moving through the dark hallway, Louise reached the phone just as Jane picked it up.

"Hello?"

After several seconds, Louise could no longer contain herself. "Who is it?" she whispered.

Jane held up her hand to ask for quiet and scrunched up her face in concentration. "Yes? Given this number by *whom*?"

Alice joined them. "Who is it?" she asked Louise in a whisper. "Is something wrong?" Louise put her finger to her lips to relay Jane's request for silence. Undeterred, Alice said, "Is it the hospital?"

"The hospital," Louise repeated with relief. "That's probably it."

Jane shushed her sisters one more time. "Ned

Arnold? You'll have to excuse me. It's late, I'm sleepy and there are people here talking into my other ear." She shot the sisters a reproving look. "Did you just ask for Ned Arnold?"

"Ned?" Alice looked from Jane to Louise.

At last Jane covered the mouthpiece and lowered it below her chin. "It's someone with an alarm company that does security at the drugstore. They say there's a problem down at Parker's and they need Ned there immediately."

"I'll wake him." Alice turned and started down the stairs toward the room they had given Ned, asking as she went, "Do they want to speak to him first or should I tell him just to go down?"

"Do you need to speak to him?" Jane lowered the receiver again and called out, "They want speak to him, but they think he'll have to go down no matter what."

Everything happened fast after that. Ned appeared in a navy robe over striped pajamas, wearing one suede house shoe and one leather loafer. He took the phone, looking groggy and grumpy about the inconvenience. Inconvenience quickly turned to shock and then dismay as he listened to the speaker, then cut the conversation short with a quick, "Call the police just in case. I'll be right there."

He rushed toward the stairs and his room muttering the words "break-in" and lamenting that he couldn't believe this would happen "on my watch."

In what seemed like seconds, he was dressed, presumably wearing the proper shoes, and out the door.

Jane wondered if they should go with him, but Louise made a convincing argument not to. "What if it really is a criminal break-in?" She had asked. "We'd put ourselves in danger or at the very least get in the way."

"A criminal break-in? In Acorn Hill?" Jane scoffed as they had headed to the kitchen to make some tea. None of them felt that she would fall asleep until Ned had safely returned and told them what had happened.

"It's a drugstore, Jane." Louise had taken her usual seat at the table as Alice tended to the tea making.

Louise didn't confess it, but she was glad that Alice had volunteered to make the tea. Louise was afraid that had she tried to do so, her trembling hands would have scattered the loose tea leaves over the counter.

Jane offered to make a snack, but none of them had an appetite.

A break-in! Louise thought. *In Acorn Hill, where I've always felt so safe and secure.* That was the kind of change Louise could do without. "There are things inside drugstores that criminals very much want to get their hands on. Why do you think Chuck has an alarm system like that anyway? He knows the risks of having narcotics and the like on the premises."

"They have an alarm because the law requires it." Alice went about preparing the tea with her usual calm and cheery nature. "If you have certain drugs or chemicals on the premises, you're required by law to have an alarm system with a manned response."

"A what?" asked Louise.

"Someone has to follow up. The alarm system can't just be a loud bell," Jane said, then her expression went pensive. "Oh, the *bell*."

"The bell?" Louise squinted in the dim light. So far the sisters' movements and whispering had not roused Heather Ann or her aunt, but they had chosen to use only the table lamp in the kitchen rather than to flood the room with overhead lights. "What about the bell, Jane?"

"Well, if there was a forced entry, I wonder if they broke the little bell that hangs over the door." She frowned and sank into a seat. "I know it's nothing compared to breaking into the pharmacy, but if they broke that bell it would break my heart a little too."

Louise thought about that remnant from their childhoods. She, too, hoped with all her heart that the little old bell was still intact.

Alice brought them their tea and sat down. They waited . . . and waited . . . and waited.

Finally Alice, stifling a yawn, pointed out, "You know, if there had been a serious crime committed, we would have heard the police siren."

144

Acorn Hill was a small town, but it did have a police department, and that police department did have a car with a siren. And none of the sisters doubted for one moment that the officer on duty would not want to miss his one chance, outside of the yearly safety demonstration at the grade school, to run that siren and turn on the red and blue flashing lights.

"She has a point," Jane said, already half-asleep. "I'm going back to bed."

She was mumbling something about needing her beauty rest when the front door opened.

Together they rushed to greet Ned.

Looking weary and a bit shaken, he smiled weakly and gave a wave of his hand. "It's all right, ladies. It was nothing."

"The alarm company called you out in the middle of the night for nothing?" Jane folded her arms over her new pink chenille robe with an embroidered bacon-and-egg design.

"That's their job. To alert someone if there is a potential problem." He shuffled his feet and even in the low light, it was plain that he had, indeed, worn matching shoes. "This time there was potential but no real problem."

"What does that mean?" Jane asked, covering her mouth to hide her yawn.

"It means . . ." Ned seemed preoccupied with his coat buttons.

Louise could tell by his posture and his hesitance

that he had hoped they would accept his vague explanation and let it go.

"It means," Louise said, "that there is nothing to tell and we should go back to bed and forget about it."

"Forget about the day Acorn Hill almost had a break-in?" Jane chuckled softly as she obeyed Louise's suggestion and started moving toward the stairs. "Never."

"You two go on now. I'm going to go tidy things up in the kitchen," Louise announced. When her sisters had moved out of earshot, she said quietly to Ned. "Do you want some tea? Or warm milk to help you sleep?"

"No. No, thank you. I'm not sure anything can help me sleep tonight."

Just as Louise had expected. There was more to this story. "Would you like to talk about it?"

He rubbed the back of his neck a moment, his eyes shut. Then, slowly, he nodded. "Yes, I think I would."

"So it was just a matter of the wind blowing the door open?" Louise freshened Ned's tea, which he had agreed to after all. She could tell he was still too wound up to sleep and that he had not yet unburdened himself of everything that was weighing him down. "The wind isn't within your control, Ned. Why let a little thing like that bother you?"

146

"Because it was my responsibility to see to it that the door was locked. I keep going over it and over it in my mind." Ned raised one of his hands from his lap and made a churning motion, twisting his wrist as if to secure an unseen lock in place. "At first I was positive that I had locked it, but the more I try to recall the details, the less I'm sure of anything."

The sisters had come to think of Ned Arnold as more than just a guest. When something troubled him as this did, it seemed right that they sit in the heart of the home, the kitchen, and drink tea from mugs like family.

"At worst, it was a simple mistake, Ned," Louise said softly. "No harm done."

"No harm done," he repeated almost inaudibly. His hand fell into his lap again. "But the likelihood for harm was there, Louise."

He had dressed in such a hurry that he had simply pulled a sweater over his pajama top. The collar now poked up on one side and the soft brown-and-blue striped fabric bunched at the V of the sweater's neckline. He wore a pair of khaki trousers that now had smudges of dirt on the knees as if he had been down on the floor checking over every detail at the store.

He gazed across the table with his head slightly bent and his shoulders rounded. The overall effect left him looking like a kid who had lost his puppy.

Even though she was only a few years his senior,

the forlorn picture he presented made Louise want to mother him. "Don't you think you are over-stating things a bit? Harm, Ned? From a door blowing open?"

"The police officer who responded told me that most crimes are crimes of opportunity. Someone who might not otherwise have been tempted could have happened upon that open door in the middle of the night and gone inside and helped them-selves."

"I just can't imagine anyone in this town doing something like that," Louise said soothingly.

"Acorn Hill is absolutely lovely, Louise, but it's not perfect." He tipped his mug up and looked down into the steaming amber liquid. "And even very good people can be tempted."

Louise curled her fingers into the fabric of her robe. "I suppose that's so."

"And putting aside any unlawful intent, what if that wind had brought with it a heavy rain? Imagine the amount of inventory that might have been ruined, not to mention water getting into floorboards and behind the cases," Ned went on. "Imagine thousands of dollars in repair bills."

Louise rested her chin in her hand. "If Jane were here she'd say something about you being a reg-ular ray of sunshine, Ned."

"I'm just being practical, Louise."

"You are just being a Gloomy Gus," she cor-rected. "Borrowing trouble, my father would have said. Then he might very well have quoted to you from the sixth chapter of Matthew, with particular attention to verse twenty-seven."

"You know the chapter and verse?" For the first time since they had sat down tonight, he smiled, if only fleetingly. "You are quite the Bible scholar, Louise. I am duly impressed."

"Well, don't be too impressed. I was just reading from it earlier tonight. But that doesn't make it any less relevant to your situation."

"All right, then, Louise, suppose you quote me chapter and verse."

She shut her eyes and recited word for word, "Who of you by worrying can add a single hour to his life?"

"I can certainly see why you think that applies to me." He nodded slowly, then reached for the baby aspirin that she had set on the table as a reminder to give the bottle to Mrs. Hammond. He rolled the small white container with the pink and blue label on it in his hands. "But doesn't the Bible also warn us against the sin of vanity?"

"Vanity?"

"Louise. I believe that ignoring this memory problem would be the height of conceit."

"I think it's a bit soon to start calling it a problem."

"When is the proper time to acknowledge it, Louise?" He opened his hand and stared at the bottle. "When something really bad has happened?"

She wanted to argue with him that he was making too much out of a few small incidents, but she respected the man enough to hear him out.

"We spoke of all the changes that have come and gone in our lifetimes and I allowed myself to hope that was all that was going on. But it's just too easy to blame my experiences on changing technology or on having too much on my mind or on being in a new situation. In the end, the results are the same."

Louise sat back and took in a deep breath of air dampened by the warm tea in front of them. She suspected that there was more to this, but what could she do? Unless Ned wanted to share what was behind his reaction, she had no right to try to draw it out of him. Still, it frustrated her to see him in such pain over a fairly natural situation.

"We forget sometimes. We catch ourselves and correct it. Life goes on," she told him.

"For now life goes on, but what if something truly horrible happens?" He shook his head and cupped his hands around his mug of tea. "No, I've slipped up time and again, and each time, I put innocent people at risk."

"I still think you are being too hard on yourself, Ned."

"And I am touched by your faith in me, Louise, but I'm responsible to everyone whom I serve at the drugstore. They have put their faith in me and my ability to do my job."

"What do you plan to do, Ned?"

"First thing tomorrow, I plan to call Chuck Parker and ask him to arrange for someone else to take over running the pharmacy."

Chapter Eleven

The next morning, Ned could not reach Chuck, but because the pharmacy was open on an emergency-only basis on Sundays, he was content to wait until Monday. He joined the sisters at Sunday service. He seemed preoccupied, however, and Louise noted his frown during the reading of Matthew 6 about the fruitlessness of worry.

Jane took the reading to heart and announced on the way home from church that she thought more people should be like the birds of the fields. That, she said, was her way of saying that she didn't feel like making lunch and everyone could fend for herself.

Alice and Louise agreed they would be quite content to raid the refrigerator for leftovers. Jane's cooking was so scrumptious that no one minded having a second taste of anything that was in the refrigerator, from warmed-over chicken cordon bleu to vegetarian eggplant lasagna.

It was just as well that they made that decision, because they had hardly reached the inn and helped Mrs. Hammond to her room when friends and neighbors began stopping by. Vera Humbert, Alice's walking buddy, dropped in, she said, to see those flowers she had heard so much about. The mayor came next to thank the sisters for organizing the town surveys.

"That couldn't have waited until Monday?" Jane wondered aloud after he left.

Alice laughed. "With those surveys and a visiting benefactress in the house, we've suddenly become the hottest ticket in town."

"Too bad people don't realize that our benefactress is upstairs with those surveys, and we have strict instructions not to disturb her," Jane said.

So many people dropped in under one pretext or another that Wendell, the inn cat, went into hiding. At first, he was happy with the extra attention company always showed him, but enough was enough.

Jane, who had so deftly wriggled out of making lunch, felt obliged to whip up some cinnamon-oatmeal cookies when the cookies that she had on hand ran out. Lilies of the field or no, as a good hostess, Jane was determined that there always would be something delicious to offer the folks who came through the door, even if they proclaimed they couldn't stay. Jane knew from experience that most would end up sipping some lemonade, sampling a cookie or two and chatting away with the other drop-ins.

Rev. Kenneth Thompson came by to welcome

Heather Ann, Mrs. Hammond and Ned, and to thank them for attending services.

Ned was gracious but distant and distracted. Heather Ann, who had retreated to go over the surveys with her aunt, came down long enough to tell Rev. Thompson that she had enjoyed his sermon and to thank him for thinking of her and her aunt by paying a call.

"It's we who should be thanking you, Miss Hammond," he said.

"We haven't done anything yet, Rev. Thompson," she replied graciously but with a hint of caution.

"Oh, indeed you have. You've given the people here something to think about, to dream about, to share and to anticipate. It's like an old-fashioned spring tonic."

"Is it always this busy in Acorn Hill on Sunday afternoons?" Heather Ann asked Alice after Kenneth Thompson left. They were in the dining room, where Alice was taking some cookies from the serving platter to arrange on a plate for Mrs. Hammond.

"No, usually it's very quiet around here. Many of our guests check out after church, and we generally take the day off to do what each of us pleases. Sometimes, we'll have a small group of friends over for dinner, but we never have the meet-and-greet we had here today. That was just for you."

Louise had come into the room when Heather

Ann asked her question. She added to Alice's answer, "Well, most Sundays it's calm and quiet, but there are times when Alice's girls group, the ANGELs, work on a project here because the Assembly Room at church is booked. And we have had the occasional guest draw the curious to make drop-in visits, though nothing like today. And we've had small civic and church gatherings when no other place was available."

"*Hmmm*," Heather Ann said, seeming to find the discussion enlightening. "Thank you."

She picked up the tray holding her aunt's bottled water, the baby aspirin that Ned had brought home the night before, and the plate of cookies. "I suppose I better get these upstairs before Aunt Ida decides I've run off and forgotten her."

"Heather Ann, you are so sweet to your grandaunt," Louise said as she laid a linen napkin on the tray alongside the cookies. "Keeping up with her pills alone is practically a full-time job."

"It's not work, not really. I love my family, and I know that as the last of the line, the only daughter in the younger generation, this kind of thing naturally falls to me."

"Not unlike my Cynthia," Louise said softly, wondering if this kind of thing would await her only child one day and if she would remember to cherish the time her daughter devoted to caring for her and her sisters.

"Despite what Aunt Ida thinks, she does need

some help and I am happy to provide it. She's looking over the surveys now and drawing some conclusions, but later I plan to go over them myself and to make notes and suggestions based on what I've picked up along the way."

Even though Louise wished that she could ask outright, "Are you hinting that you've got an idea about what to do with the money?" Louise remained silent.

Heather Ann looked over the tray one last time and said, "Looks like everything is here. I'm off!"

"You're later than usual with the medicine today, Heather Ann," Alice noted as she walked with her toward the doorway.

"Yes. I know. Ever since she had to delay taking her pills until we could get the prescription refilled, Aunt Ida has preferred to have them after lunch. To allow for any irregularities that might present themselves, she says."

"Irregularities?" Louise asked.

"Can you keep a confidence?" Heather Ann's eyes sparkled more with delight than with the sense she was spilling a big secret.

Both sisters promised with a quick nod that they would keep whatever the young woman told them to themselves.

"Aunt Ida so enjoyed sleeping in the other morning that she announced that perhaps she had been too rigid for too long: always taking her medicine at the same time every day, always rising at

155

the same time every morning. 'And why?' she asked me."

Louise and Alice glanced at one another but didn't try to offer an answer.

"Because, she told me," Heather Ann said, "she had just fallen into the habit of it."

"We are all inclined to that," Louise said softly, thinking of Ned.

"Yes, but she reasoned that she had formed that habit when she was responsible for overseeing the family business. At that time she had places to be and people depending on her to show up before they could do their work. But now . . ." Heather Ann, with the tray still in her hands, rolled one shoulder up in a good-natured shrug and smiled.

"Now she thinks she might like to shake things up a bit," Alice supplied with a satisfied expression.

"If there is anything my aunt loves, it's to shake things up a bit for other people. Why shouldn't she have a taste of her own medicine?"

Louise and Alice both nodded knowingly before Louise tipped her head toward the door. "Speaking of tasting her own medicine, you'd better get that to her."

"You're right. Altering the routine is one thing, not being in control of when and how she does it is quite another." Heather Ann quickly went up the stairs.

"That Ida Hammond is nothing if not flexible—when it suits her," Alice said, joking.

"I can see that she would keep Heather Ann on her toes," Louise said.

"Funny you should mention that. That's exactly where I plan to be," Jane said from behind them. She had come into the dining room from the kitchen to check on the cookie supply. She did a jaunty dance step toward her sisters.

Louise shook her head in bewilderment. She did not understand Jane's conversational segue. "Where do you plan to be, Jane?"

"On my toes. Well, actually I suspect I'll pretty much use my whole foot, both my feet, really— and most of my body as well."

"What are you talking about, Jane?" asked Alice, equally perplexed.

"Salsa dancing lessons. My first one is tomorrow evening from seven until nine." She put her hand over her midsection and wiggled. "What are you talking about?"

Louise frowned both at her sister's gyrations and at the way the conversation had sashayed out of control. Things had a way of doing that when Jane came on the scene. More so, she decided on the spot, when Jane *danced* onto the scene. "We were talking about Mrs. Hammond's willingness to adapt her schedule to her ever-changing lifestyle."

"Her lifestyle is changing?" That brought Jane's movements to a standstill.

"Everyone's lifestyle changes with age, Jane,"

157

Louise said, wondering if her sister would embrace that fact any better than Ned had.

"It sure does. Why, I suspect that when you are Ida Hammond's age, you may have to give up salsa dancing for something that puts less stress on your aging muscles and joints." Alice put her hands on her younger sister's upper arms and gave her a squeeze as she suggested, "Perhaps scuba diving."

"And you two will be there to push me out of the boat, no doubt." Jane laughed. "Maybe we can form an act? The Divine Howard Mermaids."

Louise rolled her eyes. "I was only suggesting that all people have to make accommodations as they age. I never said those accommodations should threaten life and limb."

"Jane may be on the right track, though, Louise," Alice said. "I see so many patients who just give up or who refuse to try new things. That kind of an attitude can hinder their recovery."

"So learning to adapt, revising your routine, trying new things, those things can be healthy?" Jane asked, giving Louise an I-told-you-so glance over her shoulder.

"Absolutely. I believe so. In fact, it's coincidental that we should find ourselves talking about this, because Lillian Dover was like Ida in that respect." Alice raised her hand to indicate the flowers that were now on the dining-room buffet. "She was up for anything that might give her a better quality of life for whatever time she had left."

"Speaking of Lillian Dover, have you figured out how to thank Abe for the flowers yet?" Jane asked.

"I don't really know what to do about the flowers. I believe he sent them to me to thank me for caring for his wife." Alice sighed. "Would it be proper etiquette for me to send a thank-you to someone for sending a thank-you?" she asked Louise.

"Well, it's never improper to tell someone how much you appreciate a kind and unexpected gesture." Louise replied.

"And you could tell him how lovely the flowers are." Jane pinched a browning leaf from the greenery, amending, "How pretty they were."

"Perhaps I will just drop him a little note," Alice decided. "I'm sure that I can find his address in the hospital records. After Louise's wonderful reminder the other day about how often we don't tell people what their kindness and help means to us, I can at least do that."

At that moment, the front door opened and a voice called, "Yoo-hoo! Can anybody hear me? Is the coast clear?"

The sisters hurried to greet their aunt, who stood with just her toes on the threshold.

"I heard she locked herself in her room for the day," Ethel spoke in a stage whisper.

"Mrs. Hammond is spending the rest of the day in

her room working, Aunt Ethel," Louise explained.

"Are you still running a fever, Aunt Ethel?" Alice asked. "You looked a bit flushed."

"Oh, I don't think so, dear, though I can't use my thermometer anymore to find out for sure."

"Why can't you use your thermometer?" Louise asked.

"I broke it."

"Oh dear. Were you able to get all the glass up? You can get a nasty cut on that thin glass, and what about the liquid mercury? Tell me you did not touch the mercury," Louise said. "It's toxic, you know."

Alice put a hand on Louise's arm. "Don't worry. They don't use mercury in thermometers anymore, Louise."

"But Aunt Ethel might still be using the same one she had in 1956," Louise whispered.

"Oh, I do not!" Aunt Ethel's hearing was clearly unaffected by her cold. "In fact, the one that broke is one of those newfangled digital types that beeps when it's ready for you to read it."

"Why that's very progressive of you, Aunt Ethel."

"They gave them out free at the health fair they held at that learning place in Potterston last fall," she said as if the sisters would know exactly what she was talking about.

"Learning place?" Jane asked. "You mean the Family Learning Annex?"

"I suppose I do. You remember, Alice. You took me over there to go to the health fair while you worked pumping up people by the arms for a couple hours."

"Pumping up people by the arms?" Louise asked Alice.

"Taking blood pressures. I volunteered to do that for the hospital. It was a very nice public service, the kind of thing I wish we could hold here in town. All of the participants either provided a free evaluation of some kind or giveaway items, or both."

"Yes. I got a whole shopping bag full of goodies." Aunt Ethel appeared especially pleased with herself about that. She sniffled and coughed, though she tried to disguise both as clearing her throat, before she plunged on with the conversation. "Including that new thermometer. Truth be told, this was the first time I ever tried using the thing."

"The first time you used it you broke it?" Jane gave a rueful smile.

"*I* didn't break it. It just *broke*." Aunt Ethel seemed to feel quite strongly about the subtle distinction. "One minute it was beeping and flashing numbers at me just fine, and the next it went all jumbled, showing nothing but dashes and pieces of numbers."

"I don't suppose anything happened to it between those two minutes?" Alice prompted.

"I just used it to stir the milk into my hot tea."
She made a circle with her hand in the air to
demonstrate just how she had used the instrument.

Louise shut her eyes.

Alice sighed.

Jane covered her mouth, pretending her laugh
was a cough.

"So my thermometer bit the dust but I'm fine, I
think." Ethel proclaimed, straightening her shoulders.

"Are you sure, Aunt Ethel? A cold usually takes
seven to ten days to run its course. Sometimes it
can be even longer when you're over . . ." Alice
caught herself. She didn't dare imply that their
aunt might need more time to recuperate because
of her age. "Let me use the old-fashioned touch
method to see if you have a fever." Alice placed
her hand on their aunt's forehead and on the back
of her neck, then frowned.

"Actually, Aunt Ethel, it's good that you stopped
by now." Jane cocked her hip and put her hands in
the pockets of her flowing gypsy-style skirt. "We
have been talking about having a dinner in honor
of Ida Hammond and thought it would be nice if
we could round up some people to talk about what
it was like to live in Acorn Hill way back when."

"Way back?" Ethel pulled away from Alice's
touch. She pushed out her lip and frowned. For a
moment it seemed she might announce that she
had no idea what the town might have been like in

the past, but she must have thought better of fibbing. She coughed. This time she did not try to hide it. She tugged her collar shut at the neck as if she had suddenly caught a chill. She coughed again. "You know, I think you are right, Alice. It hasn't been nearly long enough for me to be past the contagious stage. Knowing how your guest feels about germs, it would be unfair for me to come in and expose her, or any of you, to my cold." With that she turned and scurried off, calling back as she did, "Can I count on you to come to see me, Alice?"

"I'll bring a new thermometer," Alice promised.

"And I'll stop in with more homemade chicken soup," Jane added.

"She really does not like to be reminded of her age, does she?" Louise marveled.

"Well, we all have our peculiarities." Alice shut the front door. "Take Mrs. Hammond and her fear of germs."

"Now we don't know strictly if that is a peculiarity or more a realistic precaution." Louise thought about the things Heather Ann had said about her aunt. "You may recall Heather Ann did say that Ida wanted to make the trip now, even before it was fully spring, because perhaps she feared not being able to make it at all if she waited until the weather warmed completely."

"Oh dear, I hope she isn't sicker than we thought." Jane said, wrapping her arms around her waist.

"I think if she was seriously ill, Heather Ann would not have brought her on this trip, no matter how much her aunt demanded it."

Louise closed the front door. "That young woman really loves her grandaunt and wouldn't put her in jeopardy for the world. Not to mention that if Ida was on her last legs, her doctor certainly wouldn't have allowed her to travel. More importantly, he would not have faxed her prescriptions to Ned so she could stay here indefinitely."

"Ned!" Jane cried. "We ought to ask him what he knows. Just one look at her medicines and he could probably tell us exactly what kind of shape she's in and . . ."

"Ned would never do that," Alice said firmly.

"Never do what?" Ned said as he came down the stairs.

"It's not even worth mentioning," Alice said.

"But I . . . I haven't done anything wrong, I hope." His gaze went immediately to Louise.

"No, no," Louise said. "Jane wanted to ask you if you could determine Mrs. Hammond's state of health from the medicines that she's taking."

"And I said that you'd never do that," Alice assured him. "Divulge any personal information about a customer. Patient confidentiality and all that."

"You are quite right, Alice. I can't comment on Mrs. Hammond's health." He let his breath out.

"Okay, you two." Jane rolled her eyes. "Just

forget I ever brought it up. Put it completely out of your mind."

Again Ned looked at Louise, his expression concerned, no doubt as a result of Jane's innocent turn of phrase.

Alice and Jane walked toward the kitchen, but Louise hung back so that she could talk to Ned. "You don't feel one bit better about that nonsense with the alarm, do you? Not even having had a night to sleep on it?"

"I may have had a night, but I certainly didn't sleep." He pinched the bridge of his nose and rubbed his thumb under one eye.

"So you're going to call Chuck tomorrow?"

"Actually I called again this afternoon, only to learn that he can't be reached by phone for at least two more days."

"See? Everyone is stressed these days. Enough so they plan vacations around being able to be completely cut off from so-called civilization."

Ned just shook his head.

"Maybe you should think of this as a reprieve. A second chance, Ned."

"A second chance to make another mistake?" His eyes were sad, and his shoulders stooped slightly.

"A second chance"—Louise gently patted him on the shoulder—"to believe in yourself again."

Chapter Twelve

Y es, that's right. I do get off at seven." Alice checked the green numbers on one of the monitors at the nurse's station. It was Wednesday evening, normally the night that Alice met with the ANGELs. Most of the girls were on an overnight school trip, however, so the meeting was canceled, and Alice took another substitute assignment. It had been a slow shift, and Alice was eager for its end in twenty minutes. Hospital policy did not prohibit personal calls while on duty. Still, Alice liked to keep the few she did receive as brief as possible because it was the responsible thing to do.

She had a hard time getting that point across to Jane, who was describing her experiences in the salsa dancing class—in detail. Her account came complete with counting out steps and occasionally breaking into song. "My shift ends at seven, but I don't usually get out the door for another twenty minutes or so."

"Perfect!" came back the almost instantaneous reply.

"Perfect? For what?"

"For you to come by and see how much I've learned already."

The salsa lessons were offered in two ways: one lesson a week for eight weeks, or a fast-track for people with prior dance experience or natural aptitude. That class met two nights a week for four weeks. Of course, that's the one Jane had signed up for. Citing her athletic ability and experience as a cheerleader as sufficient proof that she had the necessary coordination and rhythm, she threw herself into the class. And poor Sylvia got thrown in right along with her.

"Jane, you're just on your second lesson!" Alice raised her voice even though the only actual noise was the music coming from Jane's end of the line. "How much could you have learned already?"

"Oh, you'd be surprised. Turns out I have a real talent for this stuff. I just hear the music and close my eyes and the next thing you know . . ."

"That is just grand," Alice rushed to say before her sister burst into another series of trills and cha-chas meant to simulate the course's typical dance music. "But I am at work and still have a few minutes left of my shift. You start your class in a few minutes as well, so why don't I . . ." Alice paused to try to think of what might satisfy Jane. Her eyes fell on the log book laid open under the counter. "Why don't I pencil you in, as they say? I'll put you down in my date book for a long talk tomorrow, maybe over lunch. Okay?"

A shadow fell over Alice's shoulder and a male's voice responded instead of Jane's. "That sounds promising."

"Oh!" Alice jumped.

"I didn't mean to startle you," he whispered,

holding up both his hands in a way that made it hard for Alice to see all of his face.

"*Um*, excuse me," she said to him. Able to see his face or not, she sensed something familiar about the man.

He turned his back and began to wrestle out of his coat, which didn't seem to want to let go of him.

"Jane, I have to hang up now."

"Don't end your call on my account. This may take a few minutes," he said, tugging at his sleeve. "I'm afraid I haven't worn this coat in a year. I never realized how much an article of clothing could shrink over time just hanging in the closet."

"I'm sorry," Alice told the man, torn between her curiosity about how she might know him and her amusement at this battle with his so-called shrunken garment. On the other end of the line, Jane chattered on faster than before, trying to get in all the information she wanted to share before Alice ended the call. Alice covered the mouthpiece and said, "It's my sister, she tends to be a bit . . . enthusiastic."

"Nothing wrong with that," he said, finally standing still. He arranged his coat over one arm and propped the other elbow onto the counter, so that he stood in profile to Alice as he spoke, a bit breathless from his tangle with his wardrobe. "Life is too short to be wishy-washy about anything."

Wishy-washy? Now there was a term she'd never heard applied to Jane. She held up one finger to the man, took a breath, then plunged in at the first gap between the thoughts that were pouring out of her sister and through the phone line. "Okay. All right. I will stop in and watch you take your lesson. But only for a few minutes. I really want to go home. I've had a long day."

"I was a top-flight salesman for forty years," he said, joining the conversation as if just being in the vicinity made him part of it. "National awards, certifications, recognitions. Yet I never missed a Sunday meal with my family or forgot my kids' birthdays or my wedding anniversary. People asked me how I found the time to do it all, and I always told them, God gives us all the same twenty-four hours. It's how we fill them up that makes the difference."

Alice was tempted to tell him about how the demands of her job made some of those same twenty-four hours much, much different and how that difference sometimes added up to days that felt either far too short or sometimes unending. She rubbed her temple. It didn't help that back home her evening would likely not become more relaxing. Ned Arnold, who had left a detailed message about the alarm problem for Chuck Parker and still had not heard back, had taken to moping around and carrying a notebook in which he jotted down everything anyone told him.

Be careful of the cat if you get up at night.
Bring cough drops for Ethel with you after work.

Lemon bars in fridge are for Ida Hammond's organization committee, do not touch.

If anyone casually added to any request the words "don't forget now," he underlined his note, sometimes two or three times. Alice half expected that when one of them wished the poor fellow "sweet dreams," the pleasantry would end up as a scribbled notation pinned to his fresh bed linens.

In addition, Mrs. Hammond still had not made up her mind about her gift to the town, and everyone was on edge.

"And be sure to make a fuss over Sylvia when you come, too," Jane pressed on, unaware that Alice had been participating in another conversation. "I don't want her feeling like she isn't measuring up just because she hasn't drawn the teacher's attention the way I have. Okay?"

"*Um*, yes." Alice stammered, forcing her thoughts back to the phone conversation, but distracted by the man standing a few feet away and, of course, by her job. "I really have to go now, Jane. I have work to do."

The man cocked a bushy eyebrow and made a show of peeking both directions down the long, silent hospital corridor.

Alice smiled at his having fun at her expense, hung up the phone and asked him in her most professional tone, "Now, may I help you?"

"Only if you still have that date book of yours open and can pencil in another leisurely meal."

"Oh, of course." Alice picked up a pen and a pad of paper from the desk, thinking the man meant that he wanted to talk to her about a patient's menu for the next day's meals. "What is the patient's name and room number, please?"

"Well, I'm really not very patient. In fact, if it wasn't already long past dinner hour already, I'd ask you to join me for a meal tonight."

"*You*? Would ask *me*? *To join you*?"

"By George, I think she's got it!" He snapped his fingers.

"As kind an offer as that is, I have to say thank you but no thank you. I don't go out with gentlemen I don't know." *Or with gentlemen I do know, for the most part*, Alice admitted to herself.

"Gentlemen you don't know?" He frowned in an exaggerated way. "I thought you of all people would get a reference from an old movie. And a musical to boot. You know, 'By George, I think she's got it!'"

Musical? Old movie? Her of all people? Alice strung the clues along and suddenly it came to her. "You!"

"None other." He chuckled.

"From the parking lot the other day."

"That was the last time we spoke, yes." His frown deepened, leaving a crease in his forehead just above the bridge of his nose.

Alice remembered that crease, but from where?

171

Who was this man besides her recent curbside admirer?

"You don't remember me, do you?"

"I do," she said quite honestly, "but I don't."

"And I thought for sure when you saw me in the parking lot that you knew exactly who I was. I would never have just sent those flowers out of the blue like that if I had known—"

"Flowers? Abe? Abraham Dover!" Alice extended her hand to shake his. "I can't believe it."

He took her hand but did not shake it. Instead he held it for a moment, turning it palm down and then laying his other hand over it. "Hello again, Nurse Howard," he said softly.

She wanted to move a few steps to put the workstation between them, but a wistful sadness in his eyes touched her heart and she stayed in place. "Hello, Mr. Dover. I wanted to, that is, I've been meaning to, or rather, I wasn't sure how to contact you to thank you for the lovely flowers."

"No need for you to thank *me*. As I said on the card, they were just a small token of thanks for all the care you gave Lillian."

"Is *that* what the card said?" she asked, trying to imagine those words in the blurred scrawl. "The card got soaked by accident, and I couldn't read the message."

"Oh dear!" He rocked back, and the movement gave Alice the opportunity to glide her hand free of his.

She tucked both hands into the pockets of her uniform. "The florist gave us your name, and my sister picked up on your hidden message."

He stroked his knuckles down his full, ruddy cheek. Crinkles of concern formed at the corners of his eyes. "Hidden message?"

"The lily," she said softly, almost reverently.

His whole face brightened. "Well, I didn't consciously intend to send a message, but I'm glad you figured out who sent them. Maybe fate just stepped in."

"Er . . . maybe, anyway, thank you. It was a lovely gesture and a beautiful arrangement."

"No, thank *you*." He dropped his hand to the top of the nurses' station with a firm smack. "When I came by the other day to make my last payment on the hospital bill and saw you taking such joy in a minor moment of your everyday life, it reminded me what wonderful care you showed my late wife."

Here in the hospital, it was so easy for Alice to conjure up the image of Lillian Dover in those last days. She was a tall woman, probably actually taller than her husband. By the time she had been admitted to the hospital, she was painfully thin and had lost a lot of her hair. Still, she had insisted on brushing it every day, and she slid a pair of ivory combs that had belonged to her grandmother on each side to hold back the wisps of white curls. She had worn a pink quilted bed jacket over her hospital gown, and every day she reminded the younger nurses that when you make the effort to look better, you feel better.

Alice nodded, running her hand through her own rusty brown hair and vowing to make an appointment at the beauty salon soon. "She was a very special patient."

"I always felt you treated her that way." He took a breath and let it out with an emotional shudder. His eyes grew moist, but not tear-filled. He looked at the floor, then raised his gaze to Alice again. "One special lady to another, I suppose."

Alice had absolutely no idea how to take that remark or what to say in response to it. So she took a deep breath, preoccupied herself with tidying the workstation for the next shift, and took a cue from her more gregarious sister. She began chattering about the first thing that came to mind. "Well, I am glad you stopped by, Mr. Dover. It gave me a chance to acknowledge those flowers."

"I didn't come by because of the flowers, though. I came, as I suggested, to ask you to join me for dinner some evening."

Alice hoped he had forgotten about that. But then, how could he have forgotten the very thing that had made him find out when she would be on duty, drive down to the hospital and put his ego on the line. "Again, as kind an offer as I still find it, I have to say no thank you."

"Because you don't go out with men you don't

know. I heard you the first time you said it. But unlike the first time you said it, you now know exactly who I am."

"Not *exactly*," she reminded him. "Obviously, I remember you now, but . . ." Alice was not deft at this kind of thing. She studied the man's expectant face. "You look different. Mr. Dover. As I recall you used to be more, that is, there used to be a little *less* of you."

He laughed and patted his enlarged stomach. "I know. During the time I was putting Lillian's care above everything else, even my own health, I became a regular ninety-nine pound weakling."

Alice questioned that assertion with a subtle cluck of her tongue.

"Well, maybe not quite *that* thin." He leaned his well-padded midsection against the nurses' station again and grinned right at her. "But it wouldn't have taken much of a bully to have gotten away with kicking sand in my face back in those days."

She stepped back, her arms folded. "Something tells me you are not the type to fall victim to bullies."

"Since I don't plan on taking you to a beach for a picnic, at least not until summer, I don't suppose we'll have cause to find out."

Despite her reservations about everything from the man's assertive request to her sense of loyalty toward Mark Graves and their special friendship, Alice found herself flattered by the man's charms. But not flattered enough to accept his invitation.

She was not in the market for a new gentleman friend, and if she had been, she wouldn't have chosen Abe Dover. He was sweet but not her type. "Thank you again, Mr. Dover, but I'm afraid dinner with you is out of the question."

"You haven't gone and gotten yourself married in the time since you took care of my Lillian, have you?" His eyes grew wide and his gaze dipped to Alice's left hand.

"No." She laughed, but she put her hands in her pockets again, feeling exposed by his stare. Alice did not feel self-conscious because of her single status. She liked her life the way it was. She loved the path that she had followed and felt no regret over her choices. She would have told all that to Mr. Abraham Dover, too, if she had the slightest inkling that any of that was any of his business. But as she was only going to be spending—she glanced at the clock again and then at the door where her replacement would be arriving any minute now—a few minutes with Mr. Dover and would likely never see him again, she decided to keep her thoughts to herself. "I think it's sufficient merely to say that I'm just not—"

"Right! *Quite* right, in fact. I should have thought of that myself."

Alice exhaled in relief.

"You, Nurse Alice Howard, are not the kind of woman to be wowed with flowers and whisked off for a quick bite to eat."

"I'm not?"

"Oh no. You are the kind of woman to be wooed."

"Wooed?" Alice tried to think of anything to say to that. Only one word came to mind. "Whoa!"

"What?"

"Whoa. As in slow down there, Mr. Dover."

"Yes. Precisely. I intend to, from this point forward. Dinner is too much too soon. We should get reacquainted with one another first."

"Reacquainted?" Alice winced, wondering how to convince the man she never felt that she had been acquainted with him in the first place. "Mr. Dover—"

"Call me Abe. Now that's a nice start on getting to know one another again, isn't it? Using first names?" He moved his coat to his other arm. "And do you know what's another good, even-paced way of catching up with somebody? Coffee."

Alice learned the day she had encountered him in the parking lot that the man was a talker. And Alice was a natural-born listener, so she really couldn't help herself when she heard him say something that practically begged for him to tell her more. "Coffee?"

"Don't mind if I do. We could go down to the cafeteria. Are they still serving? If not, I'm sure there are plenty of places within walking distance where we could enjoy a cup of java and some mighty fine company."

If this nonsense were happening to Louise, she wouldn't have any problem extricating herself. If it were happening to Jane . . .

Jane! Alice lifted her chin feeling quite pleased with the realization that she had, against her better judgment, already created an excuse for not having coffee with her unwelcome admirer. When she got home, she would have a kitchen confab with her sisters and figure out how to let Mr. Dover down gently. Until then, she could put him off by informing him of her salsa class commitment. "I am so sorry, Mr. Dover, but you see I promised my sister that I would drop in after my shift and watch her dance lesson."

"A dance *lesson*? You mean she doesn't share your natural affinity?" He did a little side step to demonstrate, and his coat rasped against the counter.

"I'm actually not much of a dancer myself, you know," Alice laughed in spite of herself. "I was just thinking about those old black-and-white movie musicals and got carried away."

"And carried me right off with you, don't you know?"

"No," Alice spoke softly but with firm conviction. "I really don't know that at all."

"Well, there you were, going about your business finding something to celebrate, just . . . going about your business. Seeing that? It gave me hope, you see."

"Hope? My little two-step? How?"

"Because on that day, when I paid off the last of the hospital bill, I walked out of here thinking, *It's over.*"

"The expenses?"

"The connection. Everything that had tied me to Lillian was done with. Finished."

"You had a life together. Children, I believe?"

"Three children, yes. Wonderful kids. But grown. Out of college and on their own. We raised them and let them go as it should be."

"Just because children are grown doesn't mean they still don't need their parents." She couldn't help thinking of how much she had relied upon her father even long after she was mature. People always talked about how much their father had depended on Alice, how much she had done for him, but in her heart she knew that whatever she had given him was only a fraction of all he had done for her.

"My children have married and have children of their own. Lillian and I, we had paid off our house. We worked all our lives and finally reached the age when we thought we could slow down and enjoy life. Then she got sick."

"I am so sorry, Abe." She had avoided using his first name, but now it seemed the only compassionate thing to do.

"It didn't seem fair. It made me angry with God."

"People go through stages of grief," she said.

He sniffled and nodded his head. "I know. That

didn't last long. Lillian wouldn't hear of it. She told me she had not lived a faithful Christian life only to die fearing that I would have a falling out with the Lord and not see her on the other side."

"A very reasonable and thoughtful woman," Alice murmured.

"Yes, she was. And I held onto her as long as I could, first by bringing her here when she might have preferred we take no measures but prayer."

"Oh, Abe, I never knew that."

"You wouldn't have, because after a couple of shifts with you, she completely changed her mind and decided to accept help, to try new things that might prolong her life or at least make her more comfortable in the time she had left."

"I did that for her?"

"And for me."

"You?"

"When I saw you the other day. As I said, I was walking out of here thinking that everything I had worked so hard for was finally over. My responsibilities were done. I felt like a man who had not one thing left to live for."

"And then you saw me do a little dance?"

"And then I saw you do a little dance!"

"I just don't see how—"

"I thought, *She certainly knows how to live.*"

"And?"

"And I didn't."

"Didn't what?"

"Know how to live anymore. I had immersed myself so long in Lillian's dying and in my own loss that I had forgotten how to live. I stuffed myself with food that I neither needed nor tasted. I spent my evenings in front of the television watching shows that neither enlightened nor entertained me. I slept without dreaming and I went through my waking hours without a dream to keep me going."

"And one silly flounce from me changed that?"

"Let's just say that seeing you dance when I did, with the things that had been on my mind and in my heart that day, it opened my eyes. It made me think and it made me thankful."

"Thankful?"

"To the Lord, for allowing me this day to rejoice, just as the Bible tells us to do." He tapped his open hand on the counter. "So I went home and called the florist and that pretty much catches us up to this moment."

This moment. "I really did promise my sister I'd drop in on her class tonight," Alice said gently.

"And the place where she takes this class, is there a coffee shop near by?"

"*Um*, Mr. Dover, I don't actually *drink* coffee."

"Then maybe someplace that serves more than coffee. There are other beverages out there, you know. Hot cocoa, tea, soda. I bet if you think of it you could picture a spot in your mind right now that's both close to where you are going to see your sister and where I could get coffee and you could get whatever you like."

The man really was a very good salesman, even when the product he was selling was spending time with him. She sighed and nodded.

"Great! Then what are we waiting for?"

"For my replacement to show up," Alice said with a laugh.

Chapter Thirteen

A nd listen to the music . . . and step back . . . and back . . . and stay on the balls of your feet . . . and step . . . and—Jane! Eyes forward!"

"Sorry, but that's my sister." Jane waved at Alice when she walked through the door.

The instructor reached for Jane's fluttering hand and returned it to her partner's shoulder. With a gentle tap on her arm, he reminded her to keep her posture tall and straight and to raise her elbows into what he had called the proper "frame."

Jane didn't need that reminder. She had seen so many movies about dancing that she felt she knew the proper posture instinctively. Dancing was so simple really; just listen to the music, move with the beat and . . .

"Ouch!"

Jane felt her shoe crunch down on the arch of her partner's foot just seconds before he let out a cry of pain.

"Mr. Alonzo," Jane called to Alonzo Diaz, the handsome young instructor of all the learning center's Latin dance classes. Though she thought it sounded a bit affected to address him this way, it was what he had asked to be called. She gestured with an open palm toward Milton Webb, the short, stocky forty-year-old man who had admitted he was here in hopes that dancing would help him reenter the dating scene after a bad breakup. "Milton and I are having difficulties. Perhaps we aren't well suited to one another as dance partners. We . . ."

How could she put this? We have different levels of experience? The difference in our heights makes it impossible to do the turns and spins? She certainly couldn't just blurt out the truth: Milton is a klutz. She felt sorry for the poor guy. His heart wasn't in dancing. It was just a means to an end. She suspected that somehow his feet seemed to know that.

"I agree," Mr. Alonzo said before Jane could explain further. Then he laid his hand on her back and said quietly, "Why don't you sit this one out, Jane? You can take a moment to talk to your guests, and Milton can get in some more dancing time."

Jane silently thanked the instructor with a bow of her head. Chin up, she strode to the side of the room, giving a finger-wiggling wave to Sylvia, who was called in to take her place.

There were eight students in the class. Unfortunately the group was composed of three men and five women. So at any given time one lady danced with Mr. Alonzo and another had to sit on the sidelines. Usually the one sitting out received coaching from Felicia Diaz, a beautiful young woman, who was in her eighth month of pregnancy. She only participated in the lessons from a chair on the sidelines.

Hand on her burgeoning belly, Felicia pointed to the chair beside her where Sylvia had been sitting, but Jane motioned toward Alice instead. Felicia made the okay sign with her thumb and forefinger to show her approval, and Jane's step became a little lighter.

Obviously Mrs. Diaz doesn't think I need any extra coaching, Jane thought.

Everyone had paid the same amount for the classes, and the instructors had to make a profit, not just from the current lessons, but from returning students and others who became interested in lessons through word of mouth. Jane had promised to spread the word in Acorn Hill. Keeping everyone happy and feeling good about his progress was an important part of each instructor's job. But truth be told, Jane had grown a bit weary of their going the extra mile with the men in the class, praising them and cheering their progress, even though none of them seemed to have a natural knack for dance.

"Sorry you don't get to see me in action right away," Jane said. "But stick around. I'm sure Mr. Alonzo will put me back in after he's given the men some time to get up to speed."

"Who is Mr. Alonzo?" Alice asked, her eyes fixed on the people stepping and twirling over the dance floor. "And what do you mean about the men needing to get up to speed? They seem to be doing just fine."

"Put you back in? That sounds more like my granddaughter's soccer game than a dance class," said a man standing behind Alice.

Jane was unsure which question to answer first. So she asked one of your own. "Pardon me, sir, but do I know you?"

"Oh!" Alice threw up her hands. "Where are my manners? Jane, this is Abraham Dover. Abe, this is my sister Jane Howard."

"Abraham Dover?" Jane put her hand to her chest and broke into a big, happy, spontaneous smile. "*The* Abraham Dover?"

"There may be others, but I am *the* Abraham Dover standing here right now, yes." He extended his big hand and shook hers with so much vigor that her silver bangles rattled on her wrist.

"Mr. Dover came into the hospital near the end of my shift," Alice explained, wrapping her unbuttoned spring jacket tightly across her chest.

There's a secret there, Jane thought. *The way she tries to hide, to make sure she does not reveal too much*. Jane smiled to herself. She knew things like this. Maybe one day she should teach a class on reading body language.

"*Hmm. The* Mr. Dover who sent Alice that gorgeous arrangement of flowers. I have to compliment you on your selection. The flowers were just breathtaking."

"Thank you."

"So, Mr. Dover, you just *happened* to show up at the hospital when Alice was finishing her shift?"

"Happened to show up nothing! I called ahead to find out when your sister worked next and timed my visit to coincide with her getting off duty and perhaps having a bit of free time for me."

"Really?" Behind them the salsa music blared, and Mr. Alonzo called out the steps.

Alice's cheeks went red, not with the blush of a schoolgirl, but with the familiar flush of suppressed emotions. Alice was too kind to just tell Jane in front of Mr. Dover what she felt about his surprise visit, but her red face told Jane all she needed to know.

"Well, it was nice of you to escort my sister over here, Mr. Dover. But I suspect that you won't want to hang around to watch me take a lesson." There. She had given her sister an out. "It was nice to meet you."

"And you likewise." He took her hand again and shook it. "As you say, not much point in hanging about, especially if you aren't even in the game, so to speak." He turned to Alice. "Shall we go have that cup of coffee, Alice? Maybe you can stop back in afterward and by then your sister will be up at bat again."

"Coffee?" Jane asked, slightly baffled. "You're going out for coffee?"

"We're just heading to the burger place across the way. I've had a long, slow day and I know it doesn't seem to make sense, but that kind of shift seems to dull the senses even more than a busy day. So I wouldn't mind having a little something to keep me alert on the drive home."

"But you don't drink coffee, Alice."

"Well, they serve other beverages," Mr. Dover interjected. He gave Jane and Alice each a big thumbs-up and threw in an exaggerated wink.

"You have me there, Mr. Dover," Jane said, feeling as if she should wink back. Abe Dover was the kind of person who inspired people to play along with him. No wonder Alice was having a hard time extricating herself from his company.

"Great. Okay. *Um*, do you mind if I have a word with my sister, Mr. Dover?" Jane touched Alice's elbow. "Just over here. Just for a moment. It's a sister-to-sister thing."

"Sure. Go right ahead. Don't mind me. I'll just take a gander at your fellow dancers and try to see if I can figure out how they do it. Or at least discern the rules of the game and guess who's winning."

They left him chuckling at his own joke and

sidestepped about four feet along the wall before Jane huddled close to Alice and whispered, "So?"

"So what?" Alice shot back.

"So, what's his story?"

"He's lonely."

"Obviously."

"Oh, because he looked me up? Only a desperate lonely man would ever do such a thing?"

"Now, don't be that way, Alice."

"What way?"

"Like . . ." Jane glanced around them then lowered her head and admitted, reluctantly, "like me."

Alice laughed.

"You know what I mean," Jane said, brushing her hand down her tan and aqua peasant skirt. "Don't read anything more into that statement than is really there. Don't go trying to make too much of it."

"Like you do?"

"Because I happen to be *good* at it. In this case, *you* are way off base."

Alice conceded with a nod this might be the case.

"Now, let's not get sidetracked. I only asked about him because I wanted to know what to do."

"Do? Why should you do anything?"

"Because I *can*."

Alice shook her head. "I don't understand."

"Do you want me to insist you stay put to wait for me to get another turn on the floor and hope he gets the hint that he should just take off?"

Alice took a deep breath, scanned the large room over Jane's shoulder, then exhaled and shook her head again. "I think this man is impervious to subtle messages, Jane. Likewise for hints and insinuations and even outright refusals and rejections."

"*Hmm.* Tough customer, then? Some people can be like that, totally oblivious to anything but their own perceptions of any given situation." Jane pivoted to face the couples both gliding and gyrating on the floor in keeping with the lively music. "Look at that couple over there, for example. They think they are doing so well, but really they would have been better off in the beginners' class. They would have blended in there, and their footwork wouldn't mark them as people who haven't been on the floor since disco was big."

"Jane!"

"I didn't mean to be unkind. Just saying that this was supposed to be an intermediate class, so I'm a bit disappointed that most people are struggling with the basics."

"Give them time. They'll learn. And so will you."

"Point taken. We're all just starting out, aren't we? Still, I can't help feeling a bit flattered, because Mr. Alonzo keeps using me as an example, you know, coming over to me to count out the beat and steps, that kind of thing."

"I'm sure that he is delighted to have you in class," Alice said.

Jane smiled happily. "What are you going to do about Mr. Dover?" she asked.

"I think I'll go with him now and then I can use the excuse of having to get back here before the class ends as a reason to cut the evening short."

Alice turned to head back to Mr. Dover. Jane followed but she was looking at the class, not her sister. "Great then. Go have fun, you two. And Alice—"

Alice stopped at the sound of her name, but Jane continued to walk, her eyes on the dancers. She slammed into Alice's back.

"Jane!" Alice said, turning around and reaching for Jane. But Jane was already staggering backward. Her shoes found no traction on the highly polished floor. She took one backward step, then two steps, then *plunk*. Down she went landing on one of the folding chairs that lined the wall.

"Oh my," Abe said. "That looked like that knocked the wind out of her."

"I'm fine." Jane laughed, embarrassed. "For my next act I'll do some acrobatics. You two should go now so Alice can get back here and I can show her I still have plenty of wind in my sails."

Alice looked over her shoulder at Abe. "It would take more than one wrong step and a folding chair to get the better of Jane."

He smiled. "The more I hear about you Howard girls, the more I like what I hear. Good for you, Jane Howard. Get out there and show the folding chairs of the world they will not get the likes of you down."

Jane laughed again, then stood and whispered to Alice, "Watch yourself. This guy is a character."

"He's all right. He's just coming back from the loss of his wife and is feeling his oats a bit."

"That would be fine if you two were going out for oats, but I worry about what a man like that might be like if you got him cranked up on too much coffee. He might follow you all the way home."

Abe ordered coffee for himself and hot chocolate for Alice. The place had a two-for-one special on hot chocolate to mark the last week they would be serving it until fall. But Abe cited his weight and begged off from the frothy milk-chocolate treat. He then proceeded to dump three packets of sugar and two little tubs of cream substitute into his coffee, and to order a fried pie for good measure.

Once the caffeine and the sugar hit his system, his chatter launched into high gear. He talked about his late wife. He talked about his children. He talked about the failed attempts at match-making he had experienced through his church, and why he would never go out with another woman he had not handpicked. That comment brought him around to Alice, and he began to talk about her—about them.

As if we are already a couple, Alice thought in dismay. And that's when Alice stopped talking altogether, not that she had gotten very much in beforehand.

Alice simply wasn't interested in Abe Dover as a boyfriend. She felt a genuine concern for him as a nurse and as a former caregiver to his wife, but she could not see herself seriously involved with a man so needy—and so talkative. A relationship with him would be like having a full-time job. And Alice wasn't ready to quit the job she already had. She was content with her vocation, with her single state and with the life at the inn that she shared with her sisters. And, of course, there was Mark Graves. Their comfortable long-term friendship was something she valued greatly.

"Mr. Dover . . ."

"Call me Abe. Please call me Abe. I thought we had settled all that."

She stood. "I'm sorry, but I have to go now."

"Oh?" He had checked his watch. "Yes, it's been twenty-five minutes, just as we agreed upon. What's that they say about time?"

"No time like the present?" she asked, deliberately missing his cue. She gathered her jacket and purse in order to make a hasty exit.

"No, no," he corrected her, "Time flies when you're having fun." He pushed up from the orange and white booth. In one sweeping movement he snatched her jacket from her hands and held it open for her, every inch the gallant gentleman. "And I certainly had a marvelous time tonight."

"But I'm afraid that I'm the one who has to fly." She slipped into her jacket, then stepped away from him. "It was very nice to catch up with you. I hope that you continue to think more positively. You know that Lillian would want you to enjoy your life."

"Yes, I know she would," Abe acknowledged with a solemn nod. Then his face brightened. "May I call for you again? I know that you don't live in Potterston, but I found stopping by the hospital at the end of your shift quite convenient."

"I'm sorry, but that's not at all good for me. My work is very demanding. At the end of my shift, even on a good day, I'm hardly fit company for anyone. And on a bad day, well, let's just say I imagine putting a strip of medical tape over my mouth to keep from biting anyone's head off."

"You? I don't believe it. Not for one minute."

"Please don't make me give you a demonstration," she warned, trying to look fierce while delivering her teasing threat.

"Okay. Okay. Message received." He held his hands up. "Never again will I just show up at the end of a shift. No more surprise parking-lot sock hops."

"And no more flowers, please."

"Well, I . . ."

Suddenly Alice realized the man hadn't intended to send her more flowers. Telling him not to had implied her expectations.

"Not that you would have reason to send me more flowers," she said, taking a step backward.

"A man hardly has to have a reason to send a lovely woman flowers, but honestly I did send them as a humble, and most inadequate, way of expressing my thanks for the way you treated Lillian."

Alice fussed with buttons on her jacket. "Lillian was a lovely, courageous woman, and I was honored to do what I could for her. I felt privileged to be part of her life even for that short time."

"Thank you," he said, emotion choking his words a bit. He extended his hand to her. "Let's just say good evening, and you can go and watch that dance class. Maybe you can give your sister some pointers on how it's done."

She laughed, shook his hand, murmured goodbye, then hurried off.

When she arrived at the learning center, she entered as silently as she could. She hoped to catch just enough of Jane in action to be able to say she had done so, and then, when that obligation was fulfilled, finally head for home.

She searched the couples keeping step with the music in sometimes fluid, sometimes jerky movements, but there was no Jane. Then a wave from alongside the wall caught Alice's eye. She edged along to take the almost identical place where she had stood beside her sister half an hour ago.

"Still?" Alice asked.

"Again," she said with a deep and wistful sigh.

"Too bad."

"How was your date?" Jane asked.

"It wasn't a date." Alice focused her attention on the dancers and not on her sister and by doing so only egged Jane on.

"And he knew that?" Jane cocked her head.

"Yes." Alice folded her arms. "He promised not to drop by the hospital after my shifts as well. So that's that."

"*Aww.* Too bad." Jane folded her arms, too, just as she might have done as a little girl parroting her older sister to get under her skin. "He was sort of cute."

"He seemed to like the idea of dance class, so maybe he'll begin stopping in on you." Two could play at the sister-needling game.

"I wish he would. Then the numbers would finally even out and I could get some practice in." Jane did a step and kick and wiggle. Or maybe she was just trying to shake the static electricity out of her skirt. Or had an itch she couldn't reach. Whatever she was doing, it didn't look anything at all like the movements of the couples on the floor. It wasn't ungainly . . . just . . . what had Mrs. Hammond said? "Out of whack"?

"Why aren't you out there?" Alice asked.

"Well, just look at them, Alice." Jane swept her arm out to indicate the panoramic view of the couples as she joked, "Maybe they need it more than I do."

"*All* of them?"

"I was only kidding. But standing here does give me a chance to study everyone's progress. Not to criticize but to see what I can apply to my own technique."

"For instance?"

"For instance, look at that pair." She pointed to a woman with brown curly hair, and a black-haired man with wire-rimmed glasses.

"Nice."

"Not bad, but look at the footwork. It's a little sloppy."

"Jane, did you ever stop to think—"

"Dancing isn't about thinking, Alice. It's about feeling." Jane pressed her hand to her chest, her fingers spread wide. "It's about digging deep inside, fearlessly searching your heart and expressing through movement and rhythm what you find there."

"It is?" Alice mimicked Jane's gesture and breathy voice and said, "I always thought it was about moving your feet and body to the beat of the music in order to have fun."

"People who think that way end up looking like that." She nodded her head toward Sylvia and the man Jane had been dancing with when Alice and Abe first came in.

Sylvia wobbled.

The man lunged to one side to steady her and to position her so that he could spin her around under his arm and get her facing the right direction again.

Sylvia tipped her head back and laughed, but her feet never stopped moving. And within two or three beats, they regained their composure and were in step with every other couple. The instructor and his partner came close and he spoke to Sylvia, who glanced over at Jane and nodded.

"Jane? Jane!" Mr. Alonzo crooked his finger to summon Jane from the sideline.

Sylvia stepped away from her partner, said something brief and bowed her head slightly, then began walking from the floor.

The instructor looked at Jane and pointed to the empty space where Jane's friend had stood moments ago.

"I liked what Sylvia and her partner were doing," Alice said before Jane left her side.

"So did I. She really is a natural."

"But if you think you can do better than that, I really can't wait to see you perform."

Jane made a flourish with her hand and bowed deeply to her sister. "Your wish is my command."

Sylvia came over to stand with Alice and to observe Jane clomp and stomp and stumble through the same moves Sylvia had just done.

"Is that right? What she's doing there?" Alice asked.

Jane sashayed left when all the other women went right. Even from across the room, Alice could see Jane rolling her eyes at her mistake. She quickly recovered and fell into step and did a fair job of things until her partner took her hand and swung her away, then pulled her around and around as if she were a top preparing to be launched.

Sylvia ducked her head and squeezed her eyes shut.

Alice held her breath. She had no idea what was supposed to come next, but she knew that winding things up created energy that begged to be released. And she also knew that nothing got Jane wound up like the chance to show off, particularly when her friends and family were watching.

A spin. A skid. A collision. A crash.

Fortunately no one was hurt. Alice had to hand it to Jane. She did not even seem to be suffering from wounded pride. Instead she raised her hand in the air, then let her upper body fall forward in a deep theatrical bow. All three couples involved got up brushing themselves off, most of the people laughing.

The instructor started to say something, stopped, then looked over his shoulder at his very pregnant wife.

She shook her head.

He shrugged and joined the merriment. One by one he went to each person and said something.

"He's very good about telling people what they are doing right," Sylvia explained to Alice.

He saved Jane for last, bending close to speak into her ear.

She listened intently.

Alice pressed her lips together, afraid that Jane's feelings might get hurt.

Jane nodded and kept listening.

"He's even better at gently offering suggestions on how to improve." Sylvia squeezed Alice's shoulder.

After one more nod from Jane, then a whispered question and a nod in return from Mr. Alonzo, Jane beamed brightly and practically skipped to the spot where Alice and Sylvia waited.

"And with that, let's take our break," said Mr. Alonzo. He spread his arms out, which emphasized the fullness of the sleeves of his dance shirt and made him look like some great magenta bird about to take flight.

Alice couldn't fault the man for his wardrobe, though. It was part of his job, a job he most certainly must be very good at, judging from the delight on Jane's face even after hearing his critique of her dance technique.

"Please meet back here in ten minutes." The instructor reached into his black pants and pulled free a watch. "That means five after eight. Come back relaxed, refreshed and ready to salsa!"

"Ready to salsa and to learn from the best," Jane cooed as she reached them by the wall. "Mr. Alonzo says that after the break I am to dance only with him. You know what that means, don't you?"

"I have an idea." Sylvia stole a peek at Alice,

who fiddled with a loose strand of her hair, then ventured quietly, "But why don't you tell us what you think it means?"

"I don't want to sound conceited, but I think he wants to teach by example. And because his wife can't partner with him to do that, he's chosen *me* to show everyone how it's done."

Chapter Fourteen

Tsk, tsk, Mr. Arnold, you know that cell phones are not welcome at the breakfast table," Jane said as she carried a platter of golden, crispy waffles from the kitchen. She walked behind Ned's chair and set the platter on the dining-room table.

"He's turned off the ringer, Jane," Louise explained. She was behind Jane, carrying two cut-glass decanters of warm syrup, one maple and one boysenberry. The thick, sugary aroma of the syrups rose and perfumed the air.

Louise peered over Ned's shoulder at the miniature screen on the gadget lying next to his empty breakfast plate. Then she placed the boysenberry syrup inches from the device. "He's waiting for an important call and will take it outside when he gets it." She said this half in explanation to Jane and half as a reminder to Ned. She patted his shoulder as she passed behind him again. "Our Ned wouldn't have brought the contraption to the breakfast table otherwise, knowing our policy of no cell phone calls during meals."

Ned laughed at Louise's playful defense of him. "I really do apologize. It's just that I still haven't heard back from Chuck Parker."

"You should take that as a positive sign, Ned." Louise put the other pitcher at the other end of the table and stood back, making sure everything needed for breakfast was there. "The man is on vacation. He left you in charge and has no reservations about doing so."

"I'm worried that perhaps he didn't get my message. He would have called back if he had gotten it, wouldn't he?"

"Called back? Why?" Jane did not scold but simply laid out the situation as plainly as she had set out the breakfast fare. "He knows that the door accidentally blew open and that nothing was taken or damaged. He has all the information he needs. It's not an ongoing situation. He realizes you took care of it and it's over. Why would he take time away from his vacation to rush to return that call?"

Ned fiddled with his fork. "I just think he'd be interested in how things are going at his place of business."

Louise knew that wasn't what was bothering Ned, but she also knew that he would not want to discuss the issue further at the breakfast table. Not being able to offer advice or comfort, she offered him the platter. "Waffle?"

"Yes, eat. Eat." Jane clapped her hands together. "I made a special waffle recipe for our important breakfast meeting."

Louise took her seat, laid her napkin in her lap, then tipped up her head. "Speaking of our breakfast meeting, I wonder where Heather Ann and Mrs. Hammond are."

"I'm here," came a sweet voice from just beyond the doorway.

"I'm here too. I'm almost down the stairs." A slightly scratchier, grouchier voice followed seconds later. "It just takes a while for me to make the trek these mornings."

"She's not feeling well?" Ned discreetly asked Heather Ann as she entered the room.

"She's feeling fine. It's because she's gotten used to sleeping in," Heather Ann confided with a laugh. "Says this trip back to her past has awakened the child in her and she no longer wants to abide by the tyranny of the alarm clock."

"The tyranny of the alarm clock," Louise repeated softly. "I always like to think of my alarm as heralding the promise of a new day."

"She really does," Jane said. "In fact, I recall in my childhood, sometimes when I would want to pull the cover back up over my head, Louise would come into my room singing about that very thing!"

" 'This is the day that the Lord has made,' " Louise burst forth with a line from the old pew-rattling chorus.

"What's all that racket in there?" Ida demanded as she entered the room and sat down.

"Exactly what I used to say." Jane plopped down in her seat.

Heather Ann glanced around the table. "Where's Alice?"

"She apologizes that she can't have breakfast with us this morning, but today is her day to go over and be with Aunt Ethel."

"Seems she ought to be over that cold by now," Ned noted, helping himself to a waffle. "Has she seen a doctor?"

"And have him tell her she's perfectly fine and that her nieces don't have to come over daily and fuss over her?" Jane asked. She smiled and shook her head, thinking of Ethel's tactics, then she passed the platter to Heather Ann. "Why would she want to do that?"

"I believe somewhere in the annals of Acorn Hill history our two aunts took the same seminar in family relations." Heather Ann delicately slid a waffle onto her plate.

"Well, unless they learned their roles as part of a church curriculum, they must have picked it up someplace besides Acorn Hill." Jane extended the platter next to Louise.

"There aren't many opportunities here for continuing education, you mean?" Heather Ann tented her fingers above her plate, her eyes narrowed.

"On occasion the school offers classes after

hours: CPR and first aid, babysitter certification, that kind of thing." Louise tried to think of other examples, but they eluded her.

"And Sylvia offers classes." Jane set down the platter. "Embroidery, appliqué and creative quilting, knitting, crocheting. Women drive in from all over to take her workshops, and you have to sign up as early as possible, because she can only fit so many people into her shop at one time. Acorn Hill just doesn't have the facilities here for bigger-scale projects."

"Interesting. That certainly supports my premise," Heather Ann murmured.

Louise looked at Jane. While she would never be so bold as to ask what their guest was referring to, for once in her life, Louise hoped that her fearless sister would. When Heather Ann had asked that they all gather together for breakfast to "go over a few things," she caught the imagination of all three sisters.

They had discussed the possible reasons for the meeting while preparing breakfast. Jane guessed that Ida and Heather Ann were going to make the big announcement. She thought that they were going to let the sisters be the first to know how Ida intended to dole out her money.

Alice thought that Heather Ann probably wanted to float some ideas by them, as companies do in those focus groups one hears about.

Louise admitted that she couldn't offer any

better possibilities. She was content to have break-fast and to listen to whatever Heather Ann had to say. Still, she admitted that she was more than a tad curious about the morning meeting. So now, the hour was at hand, and Ida's voice broke into Louise's thoughts.

"After more than eighty years of rising at dawn in order to prepare myself, body and soul, to face the chores that the day would bring, I have finally reached a conclusion."

"This is it," Jane whispered more to herself than to anyone else in the room.

Ned, who was politely waiting for everyone to arrive before diving into his waffle, looked up.

Louise perched on the edge of her chair.

Ida Hammond drew a dramatic breath and pro-claimed for all to hear, "I am not a morning person!"

The waiting assembly, with the exception of Heather Ann, let out a collective sigh.

Heather Ann looked around the table and saw that everyone was waiting for Ida to begin to eat. "Please, everyone, start on your breakfast before the waffles get too cold to melt the butter."

"I don't want anyone to go hungry on my account," Ida said as she snapped open her napkin and placed it on her lap. "Now, down to business."

Louise lifted her eyes from the string of rich smelling syrup she had been dribbling over the crisp grid on her plate.

"Your endowments?" Jane asked, apparently unable to control her curiosity any longer.

"My pills!" Out from the pockets of her peach and white polka-dot silk dress came one, two, three brown plastic prescription bottles, then a tissue, then a small white bottle that Louise recognized as the baby aspirin that had caused Ned so much grief.

"Aunt Ida, I thought we had decided to put your pills in the daily pill reminder box."

"Did that once, and all I got for my trouble was a lot more of the same."

"The same?"

"Trouble. And pills, if you get right down to it. Had to buy more of the same pills I'd already paid for and left behind." She fiddled with the bottles until all the labels faced her.

"They'll still be there when we get back, Aunt Ida." Heather Ann accepted the pitcher of boysenberry syrup and held it a moment with her eyes shut as if to better savor the aroma. "They won't go to waste."

"You better believe they won't. I didn't become a rich woman by throwing money away."

"Actually you became a rich woman by inheriting your money, Aunt Ida."

Ida Hammond pressed her lips together until they formed a thin, pale line in the middle of her sour expression.

"But there is one thing you got right." Heather

Ann laughed, then leaned over and kissed her aunt on the cheek. "You are not a morning person."

"I told you that," Ida groused. She allowed her niece to place a waffle on her plate, but the instant the young woman reached for one of the prescription bottles, Ida stopped her with a hand on her arm.

"Oh no you don't. I have a system," Ida croaked. "Now, will somebody bring me my bottled water?"

"I'll be happy to," Jane said. In a flash she rose from her chair and went into the kitchen.

"Is there anything else we can get you?" Louise asked.

"No, thank you. Just the water and a moment of peace and quiet while I take my pills. Then I promise to be my usual sweet, chipper self before we go out and about the town."

"Out and about the town?"

"Aunt Ida wants another tour before she makes her final decision. I have a few more things I want to point out to her as well."

What things Heather Ann intended to point out were lost when the cell phone by Ned's plate suddenly sprang to life, trembling on the table.

"Oops." Ned grabbed the device. "Sorry, Mrs. Hammond, Heather Ann. Please excuse me. I've been waiting for this call." As he said this, he quickly rose from his chair and headed for the hall and the door to the porch, where the cell phone reception would be better. Those at the table could hear his "Hello?" just before he went outside.

"What's his rush?" Jane asked, seeing his fleeing back as she reentered the dining room with Ida's water.

"The call he's been waiting for came," Heather Ann explained as she took the bottle and the napkin from Jane. She laid the napkin down, then twisted the cap from the bottle and set it on the napkin. "There you go, Aunt Ida. Now you can take your pills and stop acting like one."

Mrs. Hammond accepted the bottle and the ribbing with grace and good humor.

Ned, on the other hand, took the news that had come via his cell phone with far more energy than that. He came back into the dining room and quickly sat down while stuffing the phone into his shirt pocket and grinning from ear to ear. "It wasn't my fault!"

"The alarm?" Jane picked the waffle platter from the table. "I've got more of these warming in the oven. Let me get you some fresh, hot ones and then you can tell us all about it."

"Nothing to tell really." He said before she got out of the room. "It was the bell."

That made Jane stop and turn to ask, "The bell? You mean the alarm or the little dingy bell that hangs over the door?" She aimed her index finger downward and wiggled it to indicate the clapper inside the small old bell.

"Dingy." He mimicked her action.

"Really?" Louise conjured up the image of the

timeless fixture that she held in so much sentimental esteem. "How could a small thing like that set off the complicated string of events?"

"The chain."

"All right, the complicated *chain* of events," Louise amended her question.

Ned laughed. "I wasn't criticizing your wording, Louise. It was the *chain* that caused the, well, chain of events. The chain on the bell, that is." He held his thumb and forefinger up as if he were grasping something between them. "According to Chuck, if you close the door too hard, the bell swings up and over the top of the door on its chain. You have to flip it back down or the door doesn't close properly."

"Oh, I knew that." Jane crinkled up her nose, gave a wave of her hand and headed with the platter back to the kitchen.

"You did?"

"Everyone knows that," she called back.

He turned his gaze on Louise for confirmation.

She shrugged and smiled. "I'm afraid we're all so used to it that we assumed everyone knew to just give the bell a flick with a finger and set it right again."

"Why didn't you mention that when this all first happened?"

"Because it never occurred to me that you could set the alarm if the door wasn't properly shut."

"The door *was* shut. Or at least it appeared to be

shut, but it didn't lock because of the chain. The metal chain was in the channel where the top lock should have gone, and it completed the electrical circuit."

"So the alarm was on but the door wasn't locked, and that's how the wind blew it open?" Louise could see it all in her mind's eye. What's more, she could tell that Ned could do the same, and with each image, a weight seemed to be lifting from his shoulders.

Ned beamed, sat down and reached for a pitcher of syrup as if he wanted to be ready the instant Jane returned with more hot waffles. "Chuck said it happened to him three times before he figured out what was going on."

Louise swallowed the bite she had taken, then dabbed at the corners of her mouth with her napkin. "If he knew it was a problem, why didn't he tell you about it?"

"Oh, he had a very good reason." Ned's eyes practically sparkled.

"What's that?" she asked.

"He forgot."

Louise laughed softly. "Happens to the best of us."

"Not to me," Ida announced.

"You never forget, Aunt Ida?" Heather Ann did not even try to conceal her skepticism.

"How can I?" The elderly lady brandished a piece of waffle on her silver fork. "I no longer have to remember anything. That's why I take you with me wherever I go, dear."

Heather Ann conceded the point with a chuckle. "Very well. Then before either of us forgets, I just have a few questions for Jane and Louise, and you, too, Ned. I'd like to have an outsider's opinion as well."

"Ned? Ned's hardly an outsider," Jane protested as she came into the dining room with the platter of hot waffles.

"I only meant that he isn't a resident of Acorn Hill," Heather Ann clarified.

"She has you there." Ned was all but crowing now at even the most insignificant comment. "And in point of fact, I wasn't enough of an insider to know about the bell."

"Yes, that's the kind of thing I was thinking of when I referred to you as an outsider." Heather Ann sat up a little straighter before she turned her attention to the rest of the group. "That's why I think Ned might be able to offer just the right perspective."

"Fire away!" He rubbed his hands together with all the zeal and self-confidence of a new man.

"It's about this endowment business." Ida pushed her plate away, her waffle half-eaten.

"Was the breakfast to your liking?" Jane eyed the untouched food, then the older lady. "Shall I make you something else? Eggs? Oatmeal?"

"Have you changed your mind, Mrs.

Hammond?" Ned asked over the top of Jane's questions.

"You are still going to be a benefactress to some deserving Acorn Hill organizations, aren't you?" Louise waited for the others to finish speaking but not long enough for Mrs. Hammond to reply.

"Yes. No. No. And definitely not! Perhaps. And I'm still up in the air." Ida gave a nod as if she had just thoroughly explained everything and went about pouring more of her bottled water into the drinking glass by her right hand.

"Yes, you want me to make you something else for breakfast?"

"You have definitely not changed your mind?"

"Perhaps you will be our benefactress?"

Ida froze with the water bottle tipped up just enough to stop it from emptying into the glass and overflowing onto the table. She raised her gaze upward and tilted her head just slightly to the left.

Louise could just imagine what was going on in that still-sharp but morning-muddled mind.

Finally she plunked the bottle down on the table and raised her age-gnarled fingers to tick off the answers in proper order. "Yes, I liked the breakfast."

Jane visibly relaxed.

"But with this whole new discovery of my not being a morning person, I have given myself permission also to not be much of a breakfast person as well."

"Ahh." Jane nodded.

"So you can probably surmise the rest of my answers were no to making something else. No to eggs. And definitely no to oatmeal. Why young people think old people suddenly wake up one morning and decide they like oatmeal is beyond me. Can't stand the stuff. Slimy, to my palate, and totally and utterly without any discernable flavor except for the sugar you have to put on it to get it to slide down your throat."

"Not the way I make it," Jane protested. "I start with—"

Louise cleared her throat.

"I'll make some before you go just to give you a taste, no pressure."

"It's a deal," Ida said as firmly as if she were in a board meeting. "As for the rest of the questions . . ."

Ned and Louise both leaned in as if without that fraction of an inch they might miss something vital.

"As for the rest of the questions, all I can say is that perhaps I have changed my mind. I don't know my mind on the issue yet, so I am not prepared to proclaim that I have changed it. But perhaps."

Ida Hammond's declaration left the rest of them speechless.

"Which is why I said that, in regard to endowing worthy causes in Acorn Hill, I am still up in the air." She took a sip of water, then set the glass down in a way that implied, "The queen has spoken."

But what had she said, exactly?

"Mrs. Hammond, I'm confused . . ."

"No doubt." Ida patted Jane's hand.

"Let me clarify as best I can." Heather Ann dabbed at her mouth with her napkin, then placed it next to her empty plate. "I asked you all here to answer a few questions. Two really, but I want you to think about them. Don't give me an answer right away."

"We're going out and about today, you see." Ida gripped her cane at the side of her chair and tapped the tip of it on the floor. "So there is no rush. You may give us the answers to these two questions this evening when we return. Or perhaps we will meet again over breakfast tomorrow."

"And those questions would be?" Louise did not like to be kept in suspense, especially when the suspense was simply for dramatic effect.

Ida gave a nod to Heather Ann.

Heather Ann raised her chin, eyed the gathering and said, "If you were the one with a million dollars to donate in Acorn Hill, what would you do?"

"A million!" Jane murmured spontaneously.

Ned reached for the notepad in his pocket, but before he could flip the cover open Heather Ann said, "Please, no notes. I want what we discuss here to remain confidential. Between us, and Alice, of course."

"Certainly," Ned said and tucked the pad away. "Not likely I'll forget that anyway. A million dollars."

"Granted, it's a lot of money to an individual." Ida held up her hand to keep any further remarks at bay. "But unlike the miracle of the loaves and fishes performed by Christ our Lord, when money is divided among many, it tends to feed less and less."

"You said you had two questions?" Jane prompted.

Heather Ann tapped her handsome gold pen on her notepad, giving her a professional air that seemed out of place at the inn's breakfast table. "If you loved Acorn Hill for its people, its sense of community, the ambience, the foundation it had given you and the way it had welcomed you into its heart . . ."

"No *if* about that," Jane was quick to say.

"We do," Louise confirmed.

"We *all* do," Ned added.

"Yes, of course." Heather Ann folded her hands primly in her lap. "I was just trying to keep this in the hypothetical arena."

"Oh, dear no. We're not thinking of building an arena now, are we?" Ida harrumphed and sat back in her chair looking more like a sulking eight-year-old who didn't want to share her candy than a wealthy octogenarian businesswoman about to part with a million dollars.

"No, Aunt Ida—"

"Because I think your idea of one building is quite enough."

"Aunt Ida, please." Heather Ann put her fingers to her lips. "We are here to collect ideas, not plant them."

But it was too late. Louise was already wondering what Ida meant about the one building. She thought she might be able to guess, but she was excited and curious to hear what the others would come up with when left to ponder the second question.

"If you, who love Acorn Hill, believed that you might never see it again, if you wanted to both show how this place had made its mark on you and in turn make a little mark of your own on it, one that celebrates and sustains what makes this place dear to you, what kind of legacy would you want to leave?"

Chapter Fifteen

A mill—"

"*Uh-uh.*" Alice wagged her finger at Jane, then touched her finger to her ear. Her motions set the porch swing swaying. "Don't say that number out loud here on the porch where anyone might hear it."

"You think Aunt Ethel is sneaking around under the floorboards?" Jane lifted one foot and then the other as if to avoid tromping on some small scurrying presence. "We have it on the best of authority that she isn't. You left her fed and pampered and sound asleep not ten minutes ago."

"I'm not worried about her," Louise chimed in. "Ever since Heather Ann and Mrs. Hammond arrived with their big news, people prick up their ears when they are anywhere close to Grace Chapel Inn." She drummed her fingers on the arm of the white wicker chair.

"What people?" Jane held her hands out to indicate that only the three of them were there.

"I don't mean now. I mean people in general. I think that as a courtesy to our guests we should not allow ourselves to casually discuss what was asked of us today." Louise's fingers stilled. "Nor should we get too comfortable saying that number aloud. It's an easy thing to let slip if you aren't careful."

"I am *always* careful."

Both sisters fixed their eyes on Jane.

"Well, almost always. Anyway, I think you're both being overcautious. We're on our own front porch. It's not as if someone is just going to appear out of nowhere."

Jane could not have timed her assertion more poorly, for she had hardly uttered the last word when a big white pickup truck pulled up into the drive.

"Hello, Louise!" called a plump woman who hopped out of the passenger side. "After my last experience with parking around here, I decided to have my husband drive me over and drop me off."

"Your husband is welcome to come inside and wait for you if he'd like, Victoria," Louise called out.

Victoria Wellstone, the woman who had been taking piano lessons when Ned's car had gone for its solo ride, said something to the burly man in overalls behind the steering wheel. Even from where she sat, Louise could see him shaking his head.

"He'd rather go roam around Fred's Hardware and maybe see if there is anyone he knows holding forth at the Coffee Shop," she called back to Louise, then she waved to her husband and began to pick her way up the walk as carefully as if she were crossing a rickety bridge. She must have noted the peculiar expressions on the sisters' faces, because when she reached the porch, she stuck out one chubby ankle and volunteered, "New shoes."

"Cute." Jane tipped her head back and nodded to underscore her approval of the high-heeled beige pumps.

"They were a gift," Victoria explained, "from me to myself."

"Ah, sometimes those are the best kind of gifts," Jane said.

Again Victoria wriggled her foot around to show off her shoes. "I got them to celebrate and wanted to break them in before this summer."

Celebrate? Summer? Louise finally caught on to Victoria's hints. "Why, Victoria, are you saying . . . ?"

Victoria smiled broadly and stood tall. "You are now looking at the head of the music-ministry department. Temporary head, of course, but you never know. If I do a good enough job, there's talk of creating an assistant's position or even job-sharing between me and the longtime music director."

"Congratulations." Louise got up from her chair, her hand extended. "I'm going to miss you."

Victoria shook her teacher's hand without much vigor. "Miss me?"

Louise dropped her hand to her side. "I thought you only wanted to take lessons until you knew for sure that you had the job."

"Oh yes, that's what I had planned in the beginning, but then after I got the job and spent a day shadowing the lady I am filling in for, I realized I still have a lot to learn."

"I see. Well, if you just tell me what kind of music you want to work on and—"

"It's not a *kind* of music, Louise. It's more like all music."

"All music?"

"I'm interested in learning more about theory and composition."

"But Victoria, that's . . ." She didn't actually want to say that those things were beyond the woman's grasp. In the golden age of education, that type of thing was taught in the last years of elementary school, but the process was terribly time-consuming and the lessons probably learned more easily when one was young. "Those things would require a great time commitment and I'm not sure why you would need them."

"Why? Because I want to give my best to my church and to my Lord. And the more I know beyond my ability at the keyboard, the more I have to offer both."

"Makes perfect sense to me." Alice chirped.

"You do write music, don't you?" Victoria asked.

"Yes. Yes. I compose. I *have* composed."

"And as long as she doesn't start decomposing she *will* compose!" Jane raised one finger in the air.

Jane's silliness had enough truth in it to make Louise stop and think. Jane and Victoria had not stopped learning. In fact, they hungered for it and sought it out even when it meant driving to another town to find what they needed. Alice had emphasized that openness to new things was healthy.

"The truth is, I haven't worked on a composition all winter."

"You're not afraid that you've lost your touch?" asked Victoria, her eyes wide.

Lost her touch? "No. I have no fear at all that I've lost my touch, but perhaps what I do feel is worse."

"What do you feel?" Alice stilled the porch swing by setting her feet on the floor.

"Content," Louise said.

"And that's bad?" Alice asked.

"It's lovely." Louise exhaled and then laughed a little. "It's a gift that has been some time in coming after Father's death, returning to Acorn Hill and starting a new business."

"But?" Jane encouraged Louise to reveal more.

"But contentment doesn't exactly spur creativity."

Jane plunked her hands on her hips. "Do you need angst and pain and chaos to awaken your muse?"

"Oh my goodness, no!" Louise threw her hands up as if to ward off any of those troubles. "And I don't think of myself as having a muse. My gifts come from God, and I use them, even when doing secular work, as a way of praising and showing my love for Him."

"Does that mean you'll use your gifts to help me improve mine?" Victoria asked.

Louise was caught. She couldn't say no. Her instincts told her that Victoria would be a challenge as a student, but then Louise acknowledged to herself that perhaps a challenge was just what she needed. She exhaled and opened the front door to usher her student inside. "Let's discuss what you have in mind. If nothing else, I can make myself available to go over new pieces of music with you as you select them for your program, and we can work on them together."

"I think that would be a wonderful way to learn," Victoria said as she went inside.

"Where to next, Aunt Ida?" Heather Ann went to the door on the passenger side of their rented car and held it open for her aunt. When Jane and Sylvia had shown Heather Ann the town, they went on foot, but Ida's previous walks had worn her out a bit. So they had been tooling about Acorn Hill, stopping and getting out to visit with people whenever the mood struck Ida.

"I think we've just about seen it all, don't you, dear?" Ida moved stiffly to the curb, squinting first left, then right as if she wanted to make sure they hadn't overlooked someplace. "Now let's show this town a thing or two."

It wasn't until Ida stepped into the street that her intentions became clear to Heather Ann.

"You are not driving, Aunt Ida!"

"Not yet, I'm not, but I *will* be."

"Aunt Ida . . ."

"Oh, indulge me this small thing. We only have to drive a little more than a block back to the inn. After seeing all these wonderful people from the Good Apple Bakery to the General Store to the . . . what was the white building with the red roof where we met that nice Viola Reed?"

"The Nine Lives Bookstore." Heather Ann

remembered distinctly because they had joked about her aunt having more lives than a cat herself.

"Nine Lives Bookstore," Ida repeated softly, her eyes practically twinkling. "You know, I have never squandered a penny of the money my father left to me or of the money I oversaw for the Hammond family interests. I always got more out of any deal than anyone expected."

"I know, Aunt Ida," Heather Ann said, unsure of where her aunt was going with that thought.

"It's the same here."

"How do you mean?" Heather Ann stood beside her aunt now in hopes of moving her toward the open passenger door and away from any notion of getting behind the wheel.

"I mean that despite the size of the gift I plan for the wonderful people of Acorn Hill, I will receive more out of the exchange than they will. I will receive the joy and peace that comes from knowing I have done the right thing."

Heather Ann placed her hand on her aunt's back and laid her cheek against the older woman's thin hair. "You are doing the right thing, Aunt Ida."

"And I am going to enjoy sharing my bounty with these good folks, you know."

"Of course you are. So why risk running one of them down or knocking over one of their trees before you get a chance to make that announcement?" She tried to guide her aunt away from the curb. "Let me drive."

"Young people are so bossy," Ida said, shaking her head. "They have to look to older people to learn the arts of patience and compromise."

By midafternoon, Jane had gone off to visit with Sylvia, and Louise had shut herself in the music room. That left Alice with some quiet time on the front porch before she had to go in to work. She had thought when she agreed to fill in for Nancy King that she would be substituting just for her grandchild's birth. But now, it seemed, Nancy also needed Alice to fill in tonight over what Nancy had called "the dinner hour" while they brought the baby home. Except in Nancy's perception of things, this dinner hour would last from five in the afternoon until "eightish." Alice had tried to pin her down more on the "ish" part, but once Nancy got talking about her objectives, Alice found herself swept along and accepting things that she could not control and getting involved in things that she had not planned on doing. It reminded her of Abe Dover and the going-for-coffee situation. That, in turn, reminded her that after her shift she could stop in to see how Jane was doing as the teacher's pet in her salsa class.

The last week had been filled with change. The transition from winter into spring had been slow at first. Then, in the last few days as they entered the second week of April, it seemed as if the whole world had awakened in color. Bunches of jonquils crowded around the bases of trees and poked up errantly here and there in the yard where squirrels must have transplanted the bulbs. Likewise, delicate purple flowers now dotted the tufts of grass along the drive. Alice thought it funny that a week ago she hadn't even known those dormant buds existed, and now here she was admiring the joy and vibrancy they brought into the daily routine of her life.

This spring, more than any other in recent memory, nature seemed to mirror the personal experiences of Alice and her sisters, and Alice couldn't wait to see what each new day would bring

Of course, there was always the danger of a late frost. She was thinking of Jane, of course, and the whole salsa dancing situation. Jane emerging as the best dancer in the class? It just didn't jibe with what Alice had seen. She hoped her sister wasn't setting herself up for disappointment. Aside from that, hope was all around, and Alice intended to savor it for as long as it lasted.

"Honk! Honk!"

Alice was forced from her reverie as Ida Hammond's car came around the corner into the drive, swerving as it went, crushing some of the delicate purple flowers under its wheels and coming to rest almost kitty-corner to the house. The door swung open and Ida Hammond slowly got out from behind the wheel.

Alice shot up from the white wicker chair. "Oh my, Mrs. Hammond, I didn't know you knew how to drive!"

"She doesn't." Heather Ann, her face pale, clambered out of the passenger seat.

"Those that aren't moving forward in the great pond of life, sink," Ida proclaimed. "I just thought this was as fine a day as any to move forward."

Alice laughed.

"I tried to talk her out of it, but since we were only a short distance away, I relented." Heather Ann held her hand up and shut the door. "Don't worry, she actually does have her license, and the state keeps renewing it, so it's all perfectly legal."

"I just usually drive to church on Sunday."

Alice cocked an eyebrow. "Well, I suppose that will make a fine selling point if you ever decide to put your car on the market."

Ida made her way around the front of the car, and only then looked at the odd angle in which she had left it. "That won't do. Better get back in and straighten that up. We can't have another incident like the one with Mr. Arnold on our first day here."

Alice cringed at the reference to poor Ned's forgetfulness. She was glad he wasn't here to be reminded. He had left the house today so invigorated.

"That's quite all right, Aunt Ida. I'll see to the car in a minute. Why don't you go inside and rest? You've had a very busy day. I would like to have a word with Alice alone, anyway."

"Is this about that surprise supper you've been trying to plan for me?"

"You know about that?" Heather Ann turned to face her aunt.

"When you are my age, it gets harder and harder for people to pull anything over on you." She walked toward the house.

"I hope you manage to act surprised when they throw open the doors," Heather Ann called after her.

"There may be surprised faces, but mine won't be among them."

"Why is that?" Alice asked.

Heather Ann looked as startled by the claim as Alice felt.

"I plan on leaving town as soon as I make my decision," Ida said. And as if they needed further proof of her determination, she entered the house and closed the door.

Heather Ann watched her aunt go inside, then shut her eyes.

"I guess I should tell Jane that the appreciation dinner is off," Alice said.

"Maybe she can still hold it to celebrate my aunt getting out of everyone's hair."

"But she will still be in *your* hair."

"And under my skin and on my last nerve . . ."

"And in your prayers and in your heart."

"Always." Heather Ann chuckled and ran her hands back through her hair. "This trip has just been especially difficult, because I can't get it out of my mind that it might be the last one we ever make together."

"I'm sure there will be many more opportunities for you two to have adventures together."

"I'm all for the opportunities, but the adventures?"

Alice sympathized with a smile. "Think of it this way: Keeping up with your aunt is keeping you young."

"Keeping up with Aunt Ida is one thing, but today something else has me worried, Alice. Something I want to share with you."

"Shall we go inside? We could use the library for privacy if you think someone might overhear us."

"No. Here is fine. I don't actually have anything to tell you so much as show you." Heather Ann reached into her purse and withdrew a pill bottle. "I scooped this up this morning when Aunt Ida left it on the dining-room table."

Alice checked the drug's name clearly typed on the label. She quickly identified it as a medication often taken with other drugs to control blood pressure. "Is there a problem?"

"You're the nurse. I was hoping you could tell me." She opened the cap and tilted the bottle to show the contents to Alice.

Alice narrowed her eyes to focus on the blue oval pill among the round white tablets.

"What is it?"

"I don't know."

"Has your aunt perhaps mixed up her medications?" Alice suggested.

"This is all her medication." Heather Ann again opened her purse and removed other bottles. She opened them one by one, but there was not a blue pill in the bunch. She snapped all the lids back on and put the bottles away, all except the one with the strange pill in it.

"What about the baby aspirin?"

Heather Ann shook her head. "Those are pink."

"Yes, but they are over-the-counter pills that she called her heart medication."

"Oh, I see. You're thinking she might have gotten a vitamin or cold tablet mixed in?" Heather Ann shook the bottle until the blue pill fell into her open palm.

Alice noted the small numbers printed on the medication and concluded that it was a common but powerful pain medication. "Has your aunt been prescribed anything for pain recently?"

"No. She had something years ago after she had knee surgery, but when I took over I got rid of everything in her medicine cabinet that wasn't current."

"Just as you should have." Alice frowned at the pill and couldn't take her eyes from it until Heather Ann slid it back into the bottle where she had found it. It was a long shot, given the way the

Hammond family dealt with one another, but Alice had one more question she had to pose, "Have you asked your aunt about it?"

"And have her blow up? Perhaps cause an incident that would overshadow the good works she's trying to do here?" Heather Ann shook her head. "I know her medication, Alice. This is something I've never seen before."

"So I suppose you're thinking . . ."

"That it got in that bottle in the pharmacy by mistake."

"Oh, Heather Ann." Alice hated to even imagine it.

"I probably wouldn't have said anything to anyone, what with it not being Aunt Ida's regular pharmacy and us having to get this prescription filled under duress and all, and from the time I've spent around Ned I know he would never . . ."

"No. You had to tell someone. You don't help anyone by keeping this kind of thing to yourself. Even if it ends up hurting someone that you think of as a friend."

"Poor Ned."

"Poor Ned." Alice moved to the edge of the porch and gazed toward town. "But even worse are the poor customers, if this has happened to anyone else."

"I hadn't thought of that."

"We have to deal with this," Alice said sadly. "Mixing up prescriptions actually happens more often than people might suspect, but it has to be addressed." Alice said firmly. "No matter how bad we feel for Ned, somebody must bring this to his attention."

Chapter Sixteen

My goodness, the place sure is quiet this evening." Ned strolled into the kitchen. "It's been this way ever since Jane started that dance class, but I thought with Heather Ann's assignment on all our minds, you and Alice would be in here buzzing about it."

"Alice had to fill in for a co-worker for a few hours this evening." Louise sat sipping tea. Ida Hammond's medicine bottles were lined up neatly before her.

"Oh. Your sister is working, and yet you're the one who looks glum. What's the matter?"

"Ned, there's been . . . that is, we found . . ."

"What is it? Is something wrong?" He put his hands on the back of one of the kitchen chairs.

"I'm afraid that something is, indeed, wrong and it involves Mrs. Hammond." She reached for the bottle with the odd blue pill in it. "I don't know how to say this without seeming to make an accusation—"

"What, Louise?" He pulled out the chair and sat down. "Please. I know you're trying to be diplomatic, but I think I'd rather you were blunt and quick about this."

"Just as I would." She pulled the lid from the bottle and tipped it so that if Ned just bent his head and looked he would see the problem instantly.

"What?" He narrowed his eyes at her, clearly hesitant to peer into the bottle.

Louise said nothing.

He took a deep breath and lowered his gaze. In the measure of a heartbeat his face went gray. His eyes searched the bottle contents not once but twice and then a third time, as if somehow the answer to this awful reality lay in there alongside the strange blue pill.

"Ned?"

He took the bottle at last and shook out the blue pill for close examination. His fingers trembled slightly as he held it up. "This is a narcotic. A very serious pain medication."

"Yes. Alice told us as much."

"Alice knows?"

"Heather Ann took it to her first." Louise hated to have to tell him that others knew, but those were the facts. And she needed to know more from him. "Would it have hurt Ida if she had taken it?"

"I'm not her physician, of course, but from what I know of her other prescriptions it wouldn't have done much but knock her out. It would have concerned us all but done no serious harm."

"Unless she was driving at the time."

"Driving?" He shook his head to show that he couldn't fathom the situation.

"Alice said she still has her license and took a turn driving the town car today."

"No." He put his hand over his eyes. "No, that could have been disastrous."

"It was disastrous to our flowers. Luckily no one else was parked in the drive—or on the walkway." Louise started to explain what she meant then gave it up, knowing Ned had probably imagined every possible horrible scene.

"Why won't people face the fact that as we age there are certain limitations we have to accept?" Ned asked with his eyes still concealed.

"You're talking about yourself now?" Louise touched his wrist.

"Yes and no." He lowered his hand finally and met her gaze. "I'm talking about why this whole memory issue has undone me like nothing has before or ever could again."

"I'm listening."

"My first job in high school was in a local pharmacy in a small town much like Acorn Hill," he said. "By the time he hired me, the old pharmacist had already been running his business for more than forty years. I can't tell you how many times friends and neighbors told me how thankful they were that I was working there to give the old man a fresh set of eyes. I didn't understand it right away, but soon after came a very hard lesson about what they meant."

Louise got up and took the teakettle from the

stove. She raised it to ask Ned silently if he wanted a cup.

He nodded and went on. "It was my job to double check orders. I went over everything from iodine to prescription medication before I'd deliver them to customers' homes. More than once I would find small mistakes. Misspellings on labels, gauze bandages sent when plastic adhesive bandages were asked for, nothing significant. And yet, it made me question what was going on at the pharmacy."

Louise dropped a tea bag into a cup, then poured the boiling water over it. She leaned back against the counter to wait for the tea to brew and to listen intently to the rest of what Ned had to say.

"I never said anything to anyone. I just went about my business correcting the things that I could as I went along. Of course, then, I didn't really know about the medications. But when given the chance, I would try to check the information on the doctor's written prescription with the label on the bottle. This wasn't always possible after we started taking phone-in prescriptions directly from doctors that we knew.

"The fall of my senior year, a bad strain of flu hit more than half the town. We were overwhelmed with requests for over-the-counter products and prescriptions, mostly for things to ease people's discomfort. Going to school and distracted by being a senior, I wasn't as diligent in checking things over as I usually was."

"That's understandable." She scooped out the tea bag with a spoon, wrapped the string around the bag and gave it a squeeze before removing it.

"Around then I delivered a prescription to the house of a friend. For his little brother. We said then that the kid was probably just trying to get out of school, and we laughed, and I assured them that the medicine would make him feel better." He took the cup from Louise and set it before him. Without even looking at it he curled both hands around it as if it were his sole source of warmth on a bleak winter evening. "Later they rushed the boy to the hospital emergency room, where he was admitted. He was in the hospital for weeks and almost died."

Louise put her hand lightly on his arm. "You couldn't have known how ill the child was when you made those jests."

"You don't understand." He raised his head at last and his inconsolable gaze bore into Louise's eyes. "The boy had been given the wrong medicine."

"No," Louise whispered.

"Without the antibiotic he needed, the flu turned into pneumonia. Having trusted me and the old pharmacist about the medicine, his parents waited far too long, thinking the medication would kick in and all would be well."

"Oh, Ned. You didn't know. You couldn't have known."

"Couldn't I? I can't say that. I knew the pharmacist wasn't competent. I should have double-checked. Triple-checked."

"This is one reason you became such a workaholic in your own pharmacies. You had to make sure everything was done properly, every detail overseen by no one but you."

"Probably." He rubbed his thumb along the handle of the cup.

"And that's why you are taking all this so hard. Why you won't accept something like a change in a bill-paying system as an excuse for a slipup." Louise understood even though she believed he was being far too hard on himself.

"I can't help thinking, if that man had simply admitted his frailties, and that he was no longer fit to do his job, my friend's little brother would not have had to suffer like he did."

"That man is not you, Ned. It's not the same thing. I know it. You are not incompetent. You simply made a mistake."

"I'm sure that the old man told *himself* that. Everyone forgets. Everyone makes mistakes. Most people did not argue, because in a small town with only one pharmacy, people are reluctant to risk losing that much-needed service."

"Or maybe they understood that people aren't perfect." Louise said.

"In those days, they called it senility. But now I believe it would have been diagnosed as

Alzheimer's," he said, his voice as distant as h[...]
gaze.

"Ned, you don't believe you have Alzheimer's!"

"No." He looked at his cup for a moment, then shook his head more firmly and sat up perfectly straight. "No. But I also don't believe I have the right to put other people at risk for my vanity."

"What do you plan to do?"

"I plan to call Chuck and insist that he come home."

Alice's hand hovered above the phone. More than once she had been tempted to pick it up and call home to see if Louise had spoken to Ned and, if so, how he had taken the news. She made a sweeping glance of the hallway. All was quiet. The census in the hospital was still down and that meant she had little to do, especially in the early evening when the patients they did have were eating dinner and receiving visitors.

She pressed her lips together to keep herself from rehearsing out loud the way she would ask Louise so that it didn't seem as if she were being nosy. Of course, no matter how she worded the query, it would come off nosy, even though she had Ned Arnold's well-being at heart.

She checked the clock. Shortly before seven. There would be a shift change soon when the eleven-to-seven nurse went off duty and the seven-to-three nurse came on officially. At this moment ney were both going from room to room as the nurse leaving for the night briefed the newcomer about each patient's care.

On a normal shift, this transition would herald the time for her lunch break. Of course, she wouldn't be eating lunch at seven o'clock at night, but for shift work they usually called the midpoint break "lunch" no matter what time of day or night it fell. But since she was only working a half shift, she determined it wouldn't be right for her to take the full half-hour break.

She checked the hallway again, then made a visual rundown of the monitors. How had Jane described hospital work? *Every day something new and interesting is waiting for you.*

Nothing had been waiting for her today. No busy workload. No mysterious floral arrangement. And no—

Ding!

The elevator's arrival on her floor cut off Alice midthought. Probably someone coming by after dinner to spend some time with one of her few patients.

The doors slid open.

Alice busied herself with a stack of paperwork, so it wouldn't appear she'd been standing there staring at the elevator for entertainment. Now where was she, she mused, fussing with the files and loose papers she'd gathered from the worktop. No work to do. No flowers. No—

238

"Hello there, Nurse Alice Howard. You look so lovely this evening it makes a man want to waltz you around the waiting room."

"Abe Dover!"

"None other." He grinned and spread his arms wide. "Am I on time?"

"Time? For what?" She checked the clock, then the empty hallway. She wasn't exactly disturbed, but she wasn't as happy to see the man as he clearly expected her to be. "I thought you said you weren't coming here anymore."

"I promised no more showing up at the end of your shift expecting you to have time for me."

"How did you even know I was working today?"

"It only takes a phone call to the front desk to ask for you. They'll say that you are working or give me the day that you'll be on at such and such a shift."

"Of course."

"I know my angel works hard and deserves to go home and put her feet up. So, I thought I'd show up midshift and we could have dinner together."

There was so much wrong with the statement that Alice didn't know where to start.

"Your *angel*?" As when trying to sort out symptoms reported by a patient, Alice dealt with the most noxious complaint first.

Abe dipped his gaze to his hands. "I suppose that was a bit presumptuous of me."

"Why, yes, it was—"

"But I just recalled the times when Lillian was a patient here and you were showing her such individualized care, like bringing in that music you had selected just for her. I used to call you Lillian's angel."

Her reply evaporated on her lips. What was she going to do? The man had obviously gotten his wires crossed. He associated Alice with the loving care of his late wife and now with his own desire to move on with life. Even if she were interested in his affections, she would want to wait for some time to allow him to deal with his loss before entering into another relationship.

If they were of a more tender age, she'd call his attentions puppy love. And just like that delicate emotion, one wrong move, a single cutting word from her, and Abe Dover would be devastated.

"So, when do you get off for your dinner break? I thought we might go down to the cafeteria. I know it's not fancy, but fancy we can save for another evening. Right now it's enough to just have some time together."

"I'm afraid I don't have the time for dinner, or for anything else." Be direct. Be sweet. Be quick.

"Oh? They did say you were only working a short shift. I hadn't thought that might meant you wouldn't get your usual breaks."

"It's true that I am not getting my usual breaks this shift, but that's not why I can't go to the cafeteria with you."

"Oh? Is there a problem? Do you already have plans?"

"I don't have plans, but there is a problem." It made Alice's heart ache to have to do this, but she simply could not lead on the man. He cared for her but, in time, he would get over it. But only with time. And the sooner she told him the truth, the sooner his poor heart could begin to mend. "I have to be honest. I'm just not interested in any kind of relationship with you."

Ding!

The elevator stopped.

"You aren't?"

"No. I'm sorry. I'm not."

The doors opened with a whoosh.

Mr. Dover cast his gaze toward his shoes.

Alice felt awful.

"Well, I got the new grandbaby all settled in and the new parents fed and here I am back at work a whole hour sooner than I expected." Nancy King walked up to the nurses' station, then tucked her purse and a fast-food sack and paper cup beneath the counter.

Abe Dover raised his head, looking startled by the blond whirlwind.

"Thank you a million times over for filling in for me, Alice." Nancy glanced at Abe and smiled brightly. "Hello there. Are you here to see a patient? I'd be glad to take you to whichever room you are looking for."

"I'm not here to see a patient," Abe said softly. "But thank you for your kind attention."

"If there is anything I can do for you, just let me know, okay?" Nancy gave his hand a pat, then turned her gaze to Alice. "I don't think I'll be needing you, Alice. If they are doing the rounds for the next shift, I'll just catch up with them and listen in, and you can go on home."

"Sure thing, Nancy. I can wait until you get back here. Take your time." Alice tried to sound cheery, but her heart wasn't in it. She was thinking of poor Abe and how devastated he had to be feeling at this moment. She came around the counter and placed her hand lightly on his shoulder. "Are you all right?"

"Yes, or at least I will be." He nodded slowly, then lifted his head high and adjusted his necktie. "As soon as you introduce me to that lovely, lovely lady. Who is she and is *her* dance card full?"

"Who is she and is *her* dance card full?" Jane rolled her eyes and laughed lightly, not at her sister but with her. She leaned against the wall to which she had once more been relegated while Sylvia took her turn being Mr. Alonzo's salsa partner. "He actually said that? To *you*? Right to your face?"

"And to add insult to injury, as I walked out toward the elevator he didn't even answer me when I said good-bye."

Jane nodded, summing up sympathetically, "Dumped."

"Hardly!" Alice said louder than she intended.

Felicia Diaz, Mr. Alonzo's wife, turned and stared at Alice, who ducked her head and went on speaking but now in a swift whisper. "You can't be dumped if you were never . . . romantically linked in the first place."

"I beg to differ."

"Jane, I'm astonished that you'd beg to do anything," Alice teased.

"I know that you want to change the subject, but I have to tell you, people who are not romantically linked get dumped all the time. Dumped by friends. Dumped by employers. Dumped by people they had hoped would be friends . . . or employers . . . Didn't you say you were worried how Abe Dover would feel when you told him there could be nothing between you two?"

"Yes." Alice glanced back over her shoulder at Mrs. Diaz, who had obviously scooted her chair closer to them.

"Because you were afraid he'd feel dumped, right?"

"I suppose I was."

Weighed down by a very pregnant woman, the chair Mrs. Diaz sat on grated against the wooden floor as she moved it closer to them.

"And being a tenderhearted, good person, you wanted to spare him that. Now you feel doubly dumped because he didn't seem to extend the same level of concern for your feelings."

Alice, proving a little too well Jane's point about her need to include and be kind to everyone, shared her thoughts with the encroaching Mrs. Diaz. "My sister, the armchair psychiatrist."

Jane frowned. "Don't most psychiatrists sit in an armchair?"

"You know what I mean. You're practicing therapy without . . ."

"A license?"

"A clue." Alice bugged her eyes comically at her sister, as if that would finally drive home her desire to drop the matter.

Jane laughed and then pressed on. "Trust me, you're suffering from a mild case of I-didn't-want-him-but-I-don't-know-why-he-didn't-want-me syndrome."

"Is there any known cure?"

Jane rubbed her hands together. "A big dose of attention from a member of the opposite sex."

Alice held her hands up. "Stop right there. I've had all the unwanted attention I care for, thank you."

"I'm not talking about *unwanted* attention. I'm talking about something positive and reaffirming. The kind of feeling I get when I'm out there on the dance floor."

Alice lowered her voice, "Jane, about that—"

"I'm telling you, Alice, you should give Mark Graves a call this weekend." She strained to keep her eyes glued to Sylvia and their dance instructor.

Sylvia had really taken to salsa after the first few lessons, and it made Jane proud to see how well both the teacher and the class regarded her. "It will do you a world of good."

Alice shook her head. "I just want to relax this weekend. I didn't realize how much it would take out of me to do these couple extra shifts at the hospital."

"Excuse me." Mrs. Diaz did not stand up to get Alice's attention but instead remained in her chair and tugged on the back hem of Alice's scrubs top. "I couldn't help overhearing your conversation."

Alice turned to the seated woman and smiled. "And I can't help but notice that you are about to have that baby, my dear."

Felicia Alonzo chewed at her lower lip. "Do you really think so?"

"When are you due?"

"Not for seventeen more days, but when I saw your scrubs and heard you mention you had been working extra shifts at the hospital, I—" The young woman cut herself off with a sharp gasp. She turned her head to stare out at the dance floor, where her husband was twirling Sylvia under his arm.

"Go ahead," Alice urged.

At that moment, Mrs. Diaz grasped Jane's hand.

"*Oowww!*" Jane cried partly in surprise and partly in pain. For a small-boned thing, the woman had a grip like a lumberjack. And she wasn't letting go.

"What's . . ." Alice knelt and peered into Mrs. Diaz's face, totally ignoring Jane's agony. "Are you having a contraction? Is that what you wanted to ask me about?"

The young woman nodded. "I went to the hospital this afternoon, but they said to go home and relax," Felicia ground out the words between clenched teeth.

"Because it was too soon?"

Her dark hair spilling over her hunched shoulders, Felicia Diaz shook her head violently. "Because they said it was false labor."

"Well, for false labor you are giving me some very real pain," Jane said, trying not to sound too wimpy about her crushed fingers.

"Oh. *Whoooo*. Okay." Mrs. Diaz released Jane's hand and took a deep, deep breath. "I was just hoping you could help me."

Alice looked at Jane, then at the young woman again. "Have you taken any classes on how to handle labor pains?"

"Yes, but I don't need to know how to handle labor pains. I need to know how to *relax*." Her big brown eyes blinked dolefully. "Like they told me to do at the hospital."

Alice smiled warmly and laid her hand on the woman's bulging belly. "I can't say for sure, of course, but I think the time for relaxing has passed. It seems to me that you are about to have a baby."

"I am?" She exhaled in a long, quaking stream.

"I am so glad to hear you say that, because if th[is] was just false labor, I don't think I could cope with the real thing."

"This is the real thing." Without taking her hands from Mrs. Diaz, Alice looked up at Jane and commanded. "Call the daddy-to-be over here right now. They need to get going."

A few frantic minutes followed. Mr. Alonzo first tried to convince his wife she couldn't be in labor because it wasn't the due date the doctor had given them. When he finally believed her, he ran to get the car keys from his office, then ran out the door without his wife. Alice got the young woman to her feet and at last the father-to-be came back for her and carefully walked her to the door.

As they went, Jane, who only wanted to be of help, called out, "Don't worry about the class, Mr. Alonzo. I can take over for the rest of the evening."

"No!" So many voices shouted at once that Jane didn't know where to look. But she didn't have to see any one person in particular to get the message. And if she had missed it, Mr. Alonzo made it perfectly clear when he waved to his students and said, "Better you all go home. And we wouldn't mind your prayers for a safe delivery."

Better you all go home.

"Better you all go home than allow Jane to lead the class for the remaining hour," Jane said softly to Sylvia and Alice as they walked to their cars parked in the street. "Tell me the truth, you two. He aid so much attention to me and insisted I only dance with him because no one else wanted me for a partner, right?"

"Oh, Jane." Sylvia put her arm around Jane's shoulders. "He was only trying to give you that push of special attention in hopes you would . . ."

"What? Not ruin the lessons for everyone else?"

Sylvia didn't answer.

Jane turned to her sister. "Tell me honestly, Alice. Don't spare my feelings. Think of me as a patient who has to know the truth of her condition before she can get better."

Alice chuckled and jangled her keys in her hand as they approached the cars. "You make it sound so dramatic. It's just a dance class, Jane. It's not life and death."

"The truth, Alice. Am I the worst dancer in the whole class?"

"Well, I haven't really watched the whole class, but, yes. I don't know why. You're usually so accomplished, so graceful and athletic."

"It's the music," Sylvia said. "I don't think you're getting the Latin rhythm."

"The Latin rhythm? Isn't that like any other rhythm?" Jane asked.

"Yes, but you have to move to it differently. In some of these dances, you are supposed to move on the downbeat, where we're used to moving on the upbeat, with the first note we hear." Sylvia hummed and demonstrated with a dance step where she waited until the second note to begr "Like that."

Jane shook her head to show she wasn't sure she understood. "I bet Mr. Alonzo thinks I'm pitiful."

"From what I could see, I suspect that Mr. Alonzo chose you for his partner because you were the one who had the most to learn. So he gave you the most attention. But I'm sure that he only thinks you are a student who has come to him to improve."

"Yes, but—"

"There is no 'yes, but.' Go home and practice. You'll feel better in the morning. I'm going back to the hospital to see how things are with the mother-to-be."

Chapter Seventeen

When Louise took her place at the dining-room table the next morning, her cheery "good morning" got less than enthusiastic, silent nods all around. Jane, Alice and Ned were already in the room and looking glum.

"I don't think I'm up to a breakfast meeting with the Hammonds," Alice said as she stifled a yawn, then slipped her napkin into her lap. "I couldn't resist going back to the hospital to find out if they admitted Felicia Diaz, the dance instructor's wife. The next thing I knew I was holding her hand and reminding her and her husband of their breathing ercises while they waited for her parents to get here. It was really kind of a funny scene with his fancy dance outfit poking out of the scrubs they gave him."

Louise smiled. "I'm surprised you didn't stay to see whether they had a boy or a girl."

"I normally would have, but a first baby usually takes its time arriving, and I just didn't have the energy for a long wait. Mr. Alonzo promised to call the inn sometime today. He'd like Jane to notify the rest of the class."

His request had shown a measure of trust and probably was meant to restore some of Jane's self-esteem. The instructor also had asked if Jane would reschedule the two classes he would miss. However, Jane's unusually grim look as she returned from the kitchen indicated that his gesture had failed to cheer her up.

"Not only can I not dance, apparently I've for-gotten how to cook. I burned the toast," Jane announced, holding up the blackened proof of her claim. "I'm afraid to look at my breakfast quiche."

"Oh, Jane, you know that toaster has been acting up. Besides, one's culinary reputation hardly rests on toast-making," Louise said.

"Do you think they'll mind if I don't stay?" Ned, who looked as if he had been sitting at the table brooding since before the sun came up, checked his cell phone screen and scowled. "I really need to get in touch with Chuck and see what arran, ments I can make regarding the pharmacy until gets back."

The group in the dining room were startled by the sound of Ida's voice. "Well, I have never seen a bigger group of Gloomy Guses in all my born days."

Ida Hammond entered the room with a huge grin on her face. "And here I am, on the verge of making my big announcement and expecting a big send-off as I head for home."

"You've made your decision? Without hearing our answers to the questions that you asked us to mull over?" Jane rearranged the linen cloth covering the basket of warm cranberry muffins and then placed it on the table ready to be passed.

"*Mull*, what a perfect word," Alice observed. "That's exactly what I have in mind for the rest of this day, mulling."

"Who is mulling?" Heather Ann came into the room carrying an overnight bag in one hand and a suitcase in the other. Setting them both down out of the way, she asked, "And what are they mulling over?"

"Our friends." Ida indicated everyone with a sweep of her cane. "They are mulling over the questions we asked."

"Oh good. I can't wait to hear their answers." She took her seat.

"But your aunt says she's made her decision, our

nions don't seem to be significant." Jane laid a
.tter knife beside the chilled butter dish.

"Oh now, Jane—" Louise began in an attempt
.o soften Jane's words, but Ida interrupted.

"Oh, horsefeathers!" Ida laughed and snapped
her napkin as she liked to do before sliding it onto
her lap. "I'm always open to new ideas. Who
knows? If you come up with something entirely
radical, it might change my mind."

"Radical?" Louise rubbed her pearl necklace
between her thumb and forefinger.

"*This* group?" Alice asked, looking around the
table with a quizzical glance at the familiar and
definitely nonradical group. Well, except maybe
for Jane.

"Why not? We have a healer. A man of science.
A musician. A . . ."

"Woman who burns toast?" Jane offered.

"A culinary artist," Ida amended.

Jane sat there with her mouth open and said
nothing.

"Oh my, this is a first. You've left Jane speechless," Alice applauded softly.

Mrs. Hammond nodded in lieu of taking an
actual bow. "The truth is, we wanted you to think
about the things we asked in order to check my
decision against your recommendations."

"Sort of an independent study." Heather Ann
gestured with one open hand.

"Well, I'm certainly looking forward to hearing

what everyone has to say and how it dovetails differs from your decision," Louise said.

"Wonderful!" Ida settled her cane against th arm of her chair. "We'll begin as soon as I find ou one thing."

Jane, who had taken out a stack of plates from inside the buffet and set them on top of it, turned and tried, "What's for breakfast?"

Ida slapped her hands together. "No. I always look forward to your meals, dear, whatever they are. As long as they aren't oatmeal."

Jane shook her head.

"All clear for takeoff there, then." Ida gave a thumbs-up sign, then began to look around the table. "But what I must know before I go on is, Heather Ann, where are my pills?"

Ned went rigid.

Louise took a sharp, silent breath.

Alice looked toward Heather Ann.

Heather Ann put her fingertips to her lips for a moment. She cleared her throat. Finally, she got up from her seat and went over to the overnight case she had left on the floor.

"I'll get your water." Alice began to scoot back her chair.

"No, you stay put, Alice. I'll go." Jane was out of her chair and halfway to the door before Alice could rise from her seat. "I have to go to the kitchen to get the quiche anyway."

Heather Ann flipped open the overnight bag. She

ted around a moment before she pulled out the ttles and set them on the table. "Here you go, unt Ida."

The room was quiet.

Late last night, Heather Ann had come to the sisters and said that she did not want to tell her aunt about the discovery of the odd pill among her regular medications. She felt that no good could come of the revelation. It would only upset Ida, and for what? Ned had already beat himself up enough, taken full responsibility and chosen to give up his life's work rather than put anyone else at risk. That was more than sufficient.

"Here's your water." Jane came in and set the silver tray on the table with her left hand while she put the perfect golden quiche on a trivet with the other.

Ida Hammond gave Jane a slow, elegant nod even as she stretched her hand out and took up the pill bottles. One by one the caps came off. She shook out a baby aspirin first and took it with a sip of water.

They all watched her.

She paused a moment. "What?"

"Nothing," Heather Ann said. "I guess we're all waiting for you to finish so we can discuss your plans."

"Maybe while we're waiting you can each tell me your answers to my—" Ida tipped one of the two brown bottles up and peered down into it. "Where is my pill?"

"You're holding one prescription, Aunt Ida, the other two are right here." Heather Ann tapped the table in front of each of the bottles.

"No, not those pills. My *pill*. I only have one them, and it's not in here."

Heather Ann looked from her aunt to Ned, then to Louise and Alice, then back to her aunt again. "This missing pill? Is it blue and oval-shaped?"

"That's the one. My painkiller. I put it right here with my blood-pressure pills."

"*Your* painkiller?" Ned gripped his cell phone in one hand and frowned. "*You* put it in there?"

"Yes. I usually keep it in the bottle with my baby aspirin, but when I ran out of those I had to move it."

"You usually keep narcotic-level pain medication in a bottle of baby aspirin?" Alice asked incredulously.

"That's my system. You can see how that makes sense, like with like. Pain reliever with pain reliever. But when I ran out of aspirin—I take them for my heart, you know—I transferred it over to my blood-pressure pills for safekeeping and I haven't had time to move it back."

"It doesn't make any sense at all, Mrs. Hammond." Alice massaged her temples. "Not to me."

"Nor to me." Ned wadded up his napkin and threw it onto the table. "In fact, a lone painkiller among any other medication is such an anomaly when your niece spotted it we could only con- e that *I* had put it in there in the pharmacy by ïdent."

"That would be some accident." Ida scowled.

"Yes, it would. A big enough accident that it had me ready to retire completely rather than risk making that kind of mistake again."

"Again?" The old woman's scowl deepened. "You've made that kind of mistake before?"

"No!" Ned raked his hand through his hair. "I am very conscientious at work, always. I've never had this kind of thing happen to me, never to my knowledge sent out a prescription with mixed pills."

"Then why would you immediately assume you'd done it?" Ida blinked at him, the very picture of wisdom and innocence.

"Because . . ." Ned cradled the cell phone in both hands now and stared down at it. "You know how it is. As we get older, we begin to forget things."

"Speak for yourself." Ida pulled herself up ramrod straight in her seat.

"Mr. Arnold wouldn't be involved with any of this if *someone* had remembered your pills to begin with, Aunt Ida," Heather Ann chided.

"Don't you be too hard on yourself for that, dear." Ida reached out and patted her grandniece's hand.

Heather Ann's mouth dropped open.

Ned laughed and shook his head. His relief was

visible on his face. "I guess I won't be as Chuck to come home or to allow me to close pharmacy after all."

"What I want to know is where did you get th. painkiller, Aunt Ida?" Heather Ann demanded "How long have you been doing this?"

"My doctor prescribed it for me. When I had my surgery. Let's see, it's been . . . what?"

"A long time ago."

"No, not that long."

"Are you still experiencing pain from your surgery?" Alice wanted to know.

"No, of course not." Ida scoffed.

Alice folded her arms, standing up for what she knew to be right. "Then you have kept that pill too long."

"I don't understand why you kept it at all." Heather Ann picked up one of the bottles and turned it so that she could read the label. "I checked all of your medications and threw out everything that didn't have a current date on it. How did you manage to hold that one pill out?"

"I told you. I keep it in the baby-aspirin bottle."

"You mean year after year, bottle after bottle, you have been transferring that single pill? Why?"

"In case."

"In case of what?"

"In case I ever needed it." She said it as if she thought she was the only sane person in the room. "That's what the doctor told me they were for, to *as needed*. I took the ones I needed and hung .o that one in case I ever needed it again."

Alice shook her head. "I have seen so much of .is kind of thing in my career."

"Older people saving medicine?"

"Not just older people." Alice folded her hands and while she answered Heather Ann, she directed her attention to Ida, trying to drive home a point. "Parents who think having some extra pills will give them a leg up on the next time their child gets ill. Young people who want to use the medicine at a later date and in ways it shouldn't be used. People of all ages who feel they paid a lot of money for the product, so why shouldn't they keep it?"

"My thinking exactly." Ida snatched up her cane and gripped the top of it with both hands.

"But there are so many reasons why that is a bad idea, I don't know where to start." Ned's voice carried both compassion and reproach. His spirit seemed lifted and his message rang clear. "Medicine loses its effectiveness over time, for one thing. And self-prescribing an old medication for a new ailment, even if it seems like something you've had before, can mask a symptom of something much worse."

"Oh dear. I never thought of any of those things." Ida dropped her gaze to the three pills laid out before her.

Alice sighed. "I tell you, I could teach a whole class on this subject."

"Funny you should mention teaching a
Heather Ann perked up.

"Not that I *would* teach one," Alice shook
head. "The way I feel today I wonder if I kn
enough about human nature to teach anything."

"That goes double for me." Jane gathered th
stack of plates she'd retrieved from the buffet earlier and set them beside the quiche. She waved her
hand over the dish, sending a delicious aroma
through the room. "Triple maybe."

"I'm still having some doubts as well," Ned
said, though he looked anything but doubtful. "I
not only misread this situation with Mrs.
Hammond, it seems I hardly even know myself
well enough."

"Oh phooey!" Ida batted the air with one age-
spotted hand. "Listen to the lot of you, com-
plaining like that about such silly things."

"We've all been going through a bit of a bad
patch, Mrs. Hammond," Ned said.

"Bad patch? No such thing. Why look at you.
You should be having the time of your lives."

"Time of our lives?" Alice cocked her head to
consider that. "Isn't that supposed to be for much
younger people?"

"Hey!" Jane, who had been sliding the tip of a
serving knife along the edge of the quiche, stopped
and glared at her older sister.

"Younger?" Ida scoffed. "How much younger
are you going to get in this lifetime, Alice?"

looked like she wanted to say something ouldn't come up with anything.

xactly!" Ida chuckled. "Take it from someone ttle farther down the road. If you are alive, no atter what your age, then the time of your life is ight now. It's all you have, after all. Make the most of it."

"But what if—"

"No buts. No what ifs allowed." Ida wagged her finger at Jane. "So you're not as young as you used to be. Who is? Besides me, of course!"

Louise laughed and the others joined in.

"So you're no longer the best at everything you try. At least you try something." Ida turned from Jane to Alice. "So men don't throw their hearts at your feet for you to trample on in the name of love. At least you *are* loved."

Alice met her sisters' gazes. "I guess that put me in my place."

"Your place is caring for others. It's a blessing to be a blessing. That man who hurt your feelings knew the truth of that statement when he sent you those flowers. So he didn't want to spend his life pining for you! Does that detract from how much he appreciated your kindness?" Ida pursed her lips and waited for Alice to reply.

"No. It doesn't."

"Don't you forget that, then." Ida shifted her shoulders in her somber gray wool suit. "And speaking of forgetting! So you forget small things

from time to time. Lost your keys. Forgot to
something home from the market."

Those weren't exactly what had happene
Ned, but they hit close enough to home to m
him sit up and take notice.

"So you make it easier to keep track of you
keys. You make lists. You go back and get what
you forgot and you keep moving forward. When
you forget how to do that—how to adapt, how to
forgive yourself your human failings—that's when
you are in real trouble, young man."

Louise had never seen Ned Arnold in love, of
course, but she thought that if he had ever looked
at his ex-wife the way he was looking at elderly
Ida Hammond right now—with eyes of admiration
and gratitude—the man might still be married to
this day.

"And you. Miss dancing chef."

Jane blinked. "Me?"

"You're feeling sorry for yourself over not being
the darling of some dance class, right?"

Jane lowered her hand with the pie server in it.
"You really do know a lot more about what goes on
around here than we give you credit for, Mrs.
Hammond."

"Yes or no?" Ida snapped.

"Yes."

"Well, why did you take that dance class in the
first place?"

"To, *um*, energize myself."

n't understand that expression. It sounds to ke you would have gotten better results if you plugged yourself into a wall socket."

Louise bowed her head to conceal her smile.

"I wanted to stir things up in my life." Jane made stirring motion in the air with the serving piece. "To get ready for the change of seasons by planting some new seeds and seeing what might sprout up."

"Ah. And did you?"

"What?"

"Plant some new seeds? Did you learn anything? Learn anything at all that you can build on?"

"Plenty. In fact, it seems I have nothing *but* things I can build on. Or rather, improve upon."

"More importantly, did you stir things up? Did you have *fun*?"

"I certainly stirred the class up, that's for sure. And *fun*?" Jane raised her eyes and looked to the left a bit as if she were watching a replay of the whole event on some screen in her mind. She smiled slightly and bobbed her head, making her long ponytail swish. "Yes. Very much. In fact right up until I learned I was the worst dancer in the class, I was having a blast."

"Congratulations." Ida bowed her head.

"On being the worst in my class?"

"On accomplishing your goal. Do you know how many people don't even have goals for themselves? Much less how few actually achieve them?"

"I hadn't thought of it that way." Jane's fac

"Live. Learn. Love and share your gift. others." At last Ida turned to Louise.

"Surely you aren't trying to bring me intc this." Louise pointed at herself, then at the oth at the table excluding Heather Ann.

"And you? You have nothing to learn from all o. this?"

"Get her, Mrs. Hammond," Jane urged with a wink thrown in for Louise.

"If you need ammo, ask her why she hasn't composed anything all winter," Alice suggested.

"Well?" Ida leaned in on her cane as if to say "I'm waiting for your answer."

"I've already thought that through and have begun the preplanning for a piece I hope to have ready for early fall. A salute to the changing seasons."

Jane applauded softly. "Brava!"

Ida joined in. "Yes, quite. I hope you stick with it, Louise."

"I intend to," Louise assured her.

"On to the questions!" Ida raised both hands.

"The questions?" Louise stopped with her juice glass lifted almost to her lips. "What do they have to do with—"

"You'll see." Ida's old eyes glinted with glee. "First question: If you had a million dollars to spend on the community, what would you do with it? Now, I don't want to hear details or specifics. We're not running a planning committee here. It's ey and I will decide where it goes. On that I am adamant."

"he queen has spoken," Heather Ann joked. ds in her lap, she turned her upper body to ce and smiled sweetly. "May we have your swer first, Alice?"

"Well, I . . . I admit I haven't given it as much thought as I would have liked, having been dumped by someone I didn't even consider myself to be involved with." Alice laughed and put her hand to the side of her head, as if that would help her think better. "I, *um*, I'm glad you don't want specifics, because I don't have them, but I do know that the cost of healthcare has become a burden to so many people, especially in a small town like this where we have to go out of town for something as simple as well-baby clinics. So I suppose I'd do something to improve the general health and well-being of people here."

"I'm with Alice there," Ned chimed in, his whole demeanor improved. "Provide funds and advertising, and even transportation for people who have to go out of town for flu shots and health fairs."

"Excellent!" Ida thumped her cane in approval.

Alice beamed.

"And you, Louise?" Heather Ann turned to Louise, her eyes bright with anticipation.

"I have even fewer specifics than Alice. Of course, the arts are near and dear to my heart, as is the need to keep current with technology, to never stop learning. So, I suppose however I spent th kind of money, I would want it to benefit th largest number of people possible."

"Very practical," Ida commented.

"And you, Jane?" Heather Ann had to twist in her chair to see Jane, who was busy slicing the quiche, serving it onto plates and passing them along to the guests.

"Me? *Hmm*." She paused with the silver pie server in one hand. "I'm not sure anyone should trust my opinion given how poor a judge I am of my own abilities, but if pressed, I'd probably spend it on something for the young people."

"Really?" Alice and Louise asked at the same time.

"Yes. Really. You know, to give them things to do, to engage their imaginations, to involve them in the community so that they will want to make their homes here."

It tugged at her sisters' hearts to hear Jane say this. When she was a teenager, all she had wanted to do was get out of Acorn Hill. And even now, sometimes Louise and Alice worried that Jane longed for the excitement of San Francisco and the life she left there. Jane's suggestion put their worries to rest.

As those at the table thought about her response, Jane passed servings of quiche to Heather Ann and Ida and said, "Please start. This is so much better when it is warm. I'll get the others theirs in a second."

da nodded, then said, "Wonderful suggestions, very one of them!" The thump of her cane seconded Ida's verbal endorsement. Then she obediently set her cane aside, picked up her fork and took a bite of the delicate crabmeat quiche. She savored it with her eyes closed. "To think, somewhere, people are having oatmeal," she said with a chuckle. Then she put down her fork and once again addressed the issue at hand: "Now how about the legacy?"

"The legacy," Jane murmured.

Ned shook his head and muttered, "Tricky territory, trying to control how other people will remember you. Maybe it's better just to do your best, admit your mistakes and fix them as quickly as possible, then leave the future to those who will live in it."

"Nicely said, Ned." Louise paused a moment to accept a piece of quiche before Jane served herself and sat down. As her sister moved on, Louise summed up her feelings on the subject. "As for what kind of legacy I would like to leave, I would consider myself a success in all things if, when I'm gone, people say about me the kind of things they say about my father. That he was a good neighbor and friend. A patient teacher. An enthusiastic learner. A loving parent. A faithful servant. And most of all a forgiven sinner."

"Hear! Hear!" Ned raised his juice glass in salute. The others followed his lead.

Jane laughed and declared, "Well, I guess t.
is no topping that!"

"No topping that indeed!" Ida took a sip from h
water and smacked her lips. "Ahhh. Which is wh
I think we have found the perfect solution for how
to spend the money I wish to give to the people of
Acorn Hill!"

Chapter Eighteen

The Lawson-Hammond Fund for Lifelong
Continuing Education." Louise repeated the
title out loud as she and her sisters stood on the
porch waving good-bye to Heather Ann and Ida
Hammond.

"It's perfect, don't you think?" Alice asked,
leaning against one of the columns and gazing
down Chapel Road toward the main part of town.
"She realized this town *is* its people, and she
wanted to entrust the citizens with the money to
provide for one another as the need arises."

"And it seems fitting that they call that kind of
thing a *trust*," Jane said. "I can't think of anyone
better to head the administration of it than Lloyd
Tynan, either. I can already picture all the good
things that'll come of this." Jane sighed and sank
onto the porch swing.

After she had made her announcement at breakfast the previous day, Ida went with Heather Ann
to finalize the details and sign all the paperwork

the trust she wanted to establish. The money would go into an account, overseen by a board of directors, which would be headed by the town mayor, presently Lloyd Tynan. Groups could then apply for grants to provide community services. The rules for the distribution of money were clearly defined. And additional money could be donated to the fund, allowing other people who cared about the town to add to the endowment. Ida had truly established a living memorial, not just to her family, but to the spirit of Acorn Hill: neighbors helping neighbors, everyone working to make life better for one another.

The sisters sat on the porch enjoying thoughts of what Ida's gift could do for the town and reveling in the warmth of the spring day that was filled with promise. The sun shined brightly. Flowers dotted the yards, and the flowering trees bore tiny white or pink blossoms.

"Well, guess I'd better head down and open up the pharmacy," Ned said as he came through the door with his white lab coat folded over his arm. "Do you ladies want me to bring anything home with me at the end of the day?"

Home. It wasn't Ned's home, but it warmed Louise's heart to know that he felt that way about their sweet sanctuary of an inn, just as it made her proud that Mrs. Hammond had never stopped thinking of Acorn Hill as home, and that her own dear sister Jane shared those feelings for the hometown she had once wanted to leave beh.

"I have a few things," Jane said. "I'll make a list. Or better yet, I think that I'll just go out la myself."

"Are you sure? I'd be happy to do it for you. Ned started down the steps, paused and waited for her answer.

"No. I'm eager to get back in the kitchen and work on an idea I had—something experimental I want to try for a potential cooking class."

Louise pressed her lips together at the memory of the jalapeño-kiwi jelly fiasco.

"Run, Ned," Alice teased. "And don't look back."

"Hey! I happen to be a very good chef, and there are very few people who don't love my culinary experiments."

"We love you, Jane. We know that your wonderful meals bring people to the inn from all over." Alice sat by her sister and put her arm around her neck. "But pardon us if we're just a little wary about the things you cook up when you get restless."

"Perhaps from now on you could do us a favor," Louise suggested as she waved at the car delivering her first piano student of the day. "Keep the hot stuff for the dance floor."

"I can do that." Jane stood and did a quick sassy step, laughed, then helped Alice to her feet. "Only next class I take, I want one of you two to join me. You're never too old to learn, you know. As long as we're alive, this is the time of our lives."

Zachary's Lemon Mousse
SERVES TWELVE

4 lemons
8 eggs, separated (use pasteurized eggs to
  avoid the worry about uncooked eggs)
½ cup granulated sugar
2 tablespoons gelatin
1½ cups heavy cream
Extra cream for whipping
Toasted slivered almonds (optional)

Grate rind from lemons and reserve. Juice lemons and reserve.

In a double boiler, combine lemon juice and gelatin and let stand ten minutes.

In a medium bowl, combine egg yolks, lemon rind and sugar and beat until the mixture is light and lemon-colored.

Heat lemon juice–gelatin mixture in double boiler over hot water until the gelatin dissolves, then stir it into the egg-yolk mixture.

Whisk cream until thick and fold into the mousse mixture.

Whip egg whites until stiff and fold into the mousse mixture.

Pour mousse into a two-quart soufflé dish. (Or use lightly buttered parchment to "collar" a smaller dish.) Chill for at least two hours.

Before serving (remove collar if used), decorate with sweetened whipped cream and toasted almonds.

This recipe can be halved successfully.

Guideposts magazine and the *Daily Guideposts* devotional book are available in large-print editions by contacting:

Guideposts
Attn: Customer Service
P.O. Box 5815
Harlan, IA 51593
(800) 431-2344
www.guideposts.com

Center Point Publishing
600 Brooks Road ● PO Box 1
Thorndike ME 04986-0001 USA

(207) 568-3717

US & Canada:
1 800 929-9108
www.centerpointlargeprint.com